THE OTHER WOMAN

ALSO BY THERESE BOHMAN

Drowned

WITHDRAWN

The Other Woman

Therese Bohman

TRANSLATED FROM THE SWEDISH BY

Marlaine Delargy

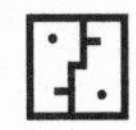

Other Press
New York

Copyright © Therese Bohman 2014
Translation copyright © Marlaine Delargy 2015

Originally published in Swedish as *Den andra kvinnan*
by Norstedts, Stockholm, Sweden, in 2014.

Other Press gratefully acknowledges that the cost of
this translation was defrayed by a subsidy from the
Swedish Arts Council.

Production editor: Yvonne E. Cárdenas
Text designer: Julie Fry
This book was set in Whitman by Alpha Design &
Composition of Pittsfield, NH.

10 9 8 7 6 5 4 3 2 1

All rights reserved. No part of this publication may be reproduced or transmitted in any form or by any means, electronic or mechanical, including photocopying, recording, or by any information storage and retrieval system, without written permission from Other Press LLC, except in the case of brief quotations in reviews for inclusion in a magazine, newspaper, or broadcast. Printed in the United States of America on acid-free paper. For information write to Other Press LLC, 267 Fifth Avenue, 6th Floor, New York, NY 10016. Or visit our Web site: www.otherpress.com

Library of Congress Cataloging-in-Publication Data

Bohman, Therese, 1978- author.
[Andra kvinnan. English]
The other woman / Therese Bohman ; translated by Marlaine Delargy.
pages cm
ISBN 978-1-59051-743-7 (paperback) — ISBN 978-1-59051-744-4 (e-book) 1. Man-woman relationships—Fiction.
I. Delargy, Marlaine, translator. II. Title.
PT9877.12.O48A5413 2016
839.73'8—dc23

2015031212

Publisher's Note:
This is a work of fiction. Names, characters, places, and incidents either are the product of the author's imagination or are used fictitiously, and any resemblance to actual persons, living or dead, events, or locales is entirely coincidental.

My plebeian blood saved me,
I do not find it very easy to die.
It is worse for the gods who must have love.
/.../
I sit in the kitchen and my heart
is nothing more than a sponge.
It has been in the depths, and can absorb
anything.

ÅSA NELVIN

NOVEMBER has settled over Norrköping, the town has been shrouded in mist all through the fall. The linden trees lining the avenues are a blaze of yellow, the air is mild but the morning is bitterly cold as I walk to the bus stop down by the station, cutting across the forecourt of the Östgöta Theater and reading the inscription above the main entrance: PROCLAIM CENTURIES OF SORROW, PROCLAIM CENTURIES OF JOY.

The floors at home are cold, the whole apartment is cold because the landlord doesn't seem to have got the heat working yet, the radiators are barely lukewarm and the place is so drafty. I live on the ground floor and there are no blinds in the room that serves as both my living room and bedroom, facing onto the street. Perhaps they were broken by someone who lived here before me. Instead I have stuck baking parchment on the inside of the lower half of the windows, letting in the light but preventing people passing by from seeing in. Before I did that I woke up one morning to find a man staring in at me, his face floating outside the window like a pink balloon. He walked away as soon as he realized I had seen him, but he might have been standing there for a long time, watching me as I slept. I couldn't shake off the idea, it was both unpleasant and titillating: perhaps he's not the only one, I thought. Perhaps he's heard about me from an acquaintance, perhaps they take turns, these men who come and watch me while I sleep, arriving as soon as it grows light and hoping that I will kick off the covers just a little bit more.

Then the feeling of distaste took over and I went and bought the baking parchment, taping it carefully to the glass, making sure it came up high enough so that no one would be able to see in, I even went outside to check that there were no gaps.

On the days when I am working my alarm clock rings at six-thirty. The asphalt outside my window is a deep black, it is a wet fall, there is mist in the air in the mornings, the smell of dampness, it comes from the harbor, or perhaps all the way from the sea.

The monotony of my morning routine is soporific, bordering on dreamlike: the bus which is always late, crawling through suburbs still shrouded in mist, following the route I have traveled so often that I have begun to recognize the license plates of the cars parked in their usual spots, the local stores with their misspelled signs offering cheap tobacco.

The woman from the Red Cross who stands in the hospital foyer with her collection box is always there before I arrive in the mornings, I nod to her, thinking that I ought to give her some money one of these days when I have change, just as I think every single morning. I switch off the alarm in the empty cafeteria, unlock the changing rooms, put on my uniform.

Those of us who work in the kitchen and the cafeteria wear the same style of blouse as the junior nurses: square, V-necked, loose, and with no attempt to actually fit the wearer, they kind of stick out from the chest, making you look enormous even if you only have a small bust. The white pants are meant for male hospital staff, but they suit me perfectly if I choose a small size, they are straight cut and fit snugly over my hips. Wearing the unattractive uniform was something I found very difficult at first, but I have ways of dealing with it: fake tan on my arms so that I don't look so pale, a few drops of perfume at the base of my throat so that I can dip my head and inhale the fragrance when the smell of food and washing up becomes too intrusive, and pretty underwear which I sometimes allow a glimpse of through the white, shapeless blouse, a hint of lace around my breasts. I think it looks sexy rather than vulgar, it is only a suggestion, a reminder that I am more than the situation in which I find myself when I am wearing my ugly uniform.

I clock in and switch on all the lights, unlock the doors and the elevators, turn off the large warming cabinet which has been on all night, I throw away the leftover trays containing roast Falun sausage and mashed potatoes. There is nothing wrong with roast sausage and mashed potatoes, my mother used to serve it up when I lived at home and it was always delicious, but nothing really tastes good from the kitchens here, nothing is seasoned properly. Everything tastes like baby food, the sausage is sliced too thickly, the mashed potato is somehow chewy.

Magdalena arrives as I am dropping the trays into the big black garbage sack.

"What's that?" she says.

"Yesterday's leftovers."

"That's disgusting – lazy jerks. Were you working yesterday?"

"No."

"I haven't been in for a week. They never call me. Do they call you?"

"I've had a few shifts this week."

"They rang me this morning, Siv is out sick again."

She ties an apron around her waist and begins to run water into the serving counters. When Magdalena is working she is in charge, even though she is employed only on an hourly basis just like me; I let her get on with it. She has worked here for a long time under the same appalling conditions, nobody is interested in employing her on a full contract, she is always scheming, always gossiping. Today she tells me that one of the cooks down in the kitchen has stolen money from petty cash, it's a secret of course, Magdalena has promised not to pass it on, her expression is challenging as she looks at me.

We take a break when we have put out everything that needs to be put out and I have washed several crates of wineglasses and a huge pile of plates—feathery strands of dill stuck to a greasy film of mayonnaise—from some event, some group that had borrowed our crockery and glassware. We always sit at the same table, right next to the window with a view over the enormous parking lot in front of the entrance to Norrköping Hospital. I often think that there should be a beautiful park out there instead, a peaceful place for patients to stroll when they want to escape the corridors for a while, or some greenery for them to rest their eyes on, but there are only bus stops, parking bays for cabs, a constant stream of people coming and going, being picked up and dropped off as the rain hangs in the air. Magdalena takes a prawn baguette out of the chill counter.

"Want to share?"

I shake my head and choose a cheese roll, badly wrapped in plastic.

"It's chicken casserole with pineapple today," Magdalena says enthusiastically, I envy her ability to summon up enthusiasm in this job. "I'm going to take a portion home for Anders, he loves it."

Then the trolleys arrive with the dish of the day, chicken casserole in huge containers and an unimaginative vegetarian stew. I cook rice in the big steamer and we portion out the food, a scoop of rice with chicken in a sweet-and-sour sauce ladled on top, then we put on the lids and stack the trays in the warming cabinet. As midday approaches the customers begin to arrive: hospital staff and a few family members, we are running out of chicken casserole. I call down to the kitchen for more supplies.

"Does the casserole contain peanuts?" one of the junior nurses asks.

"I don't think so," I say, "I can easily call up and check, just to be on the safe side."

"It might be a good idea to have a list of ingredients on display somewhere," she says, looking at her colleague, who nods and rolls her eyes, as if to say you can't expect something like that here. "I'm sure more people would like to know."

There is a strict hierarchy within the hospital, I understood that on my very first day. The junior nurses want to avoid being at the bottom of the food chain at all costs, so they feel the need to assert their superiority over the catering staff, who wear the same clothes as them but simply shovel food onto plates. The doctors have a completely different attitude, they are secure in their position, they are always pleasant in a slightly distant way, patient, polite. Some of them are stylish, impressive in their white coats with name badges stating their title, I amuse myself by flirting with one or two of them, being a little more helpful, a little more cheerful.

Occasionally I have wondered what it would be like to have an affair with one of them, particularly the tall handsome consultant who comes in for lunch all too rarely. I have thought about where we would meet, imagined him at home with me, even if the idea of him in my tiny apartment among my things is an unlikely scenario. I picture him sitting on my sofa, we are drinking a glass of wine, chatting. Perhaps we are discussing literature, which turns out to be a shared passion. I think of him as an educated man, interested in art and literature and politics, he is well traveled, well read, well bred, he would stand in front of the bookcase examining my books, impressed by what he sees. I wonder what he thinks of me, if anything at all. Does he assume I am like the other casual staff in the kitchen and the cafeteria? A young mom, perhaps, who has studied food technology at school and is now working temporarily in the hospital cafeteria as a way into a whole life spent in school canteens and mass catering, with an aching back and shoulders.

I mention him to Emelie when we meet up for a coffee in the evening. My whole body is weary, but if I don't do anything in the evenings, I feel as if my job is taking over my life, and that makes me miserable, so I usually say yes if Emelie suggests getting together.

"Oh please," she says. "How old is he? Fifty?"

"Something like that."

"Could you really do that kind of thing? Seriously?"

I shrug my shoulders, although I know perfectly well that I could. That is exactly the kind of thing you have to do if you want to write, particularly if you live in a town like Norrköping. If nothing is happening, then you have to make sure something does happen, so that you have something to write about. I wouldn't say it, because I think it sounds pompous, and I'm afraid Emelie will look at me with an expression that says, *Who do you think you are?* In spite of the fact that I have never thought I am anything special, I choose to keep quiet.

"Is he married?" she asks.

"No idea, it's never occurred to me to find out."

Emelie is drinking some kind of beige coffee mixture in a large glass through a straw, the wind is howling outside, it gets dark early at this time of year. The café is full of students, just like the town, the whole of Norrköping is full of students these days, the windows facing out onto the square steam up with the warmth of their bodies, their group projects and their gossip over cup after cup of the disgusting coffee you get everywhere here. I walk home along Kungsgatan, stop off in the minimarket where oranges are on special. Perhaps I am suffering from a vitamin deficiency, perhaps that is why I am so tired. Or scurvy, my teeth will soon drop out. I run my tongue along the inside of my teeth, perhaps they feel a little loose.

I buy three oranges. They are grotesquely large, the biggest oranges I have ever seen. The sidewalks are dark with the dampness, my legs are aching. My calves grow stiff and taut from standing on the hard concrete floor all day long, I lie down on the bed as soon as I get home, I pile up the pillows and the duvet at the foot of the bed and lie on my back with my feet raised. I can feel the blood being released from my feet, flowing through my legs, I have pins and needles in my calves. As I reach for the book at the top of the stack on my bedside table my cell phone vibrates with a text from Emelie: "Have just decided to go to bar tonight, want to come?" I reply that I am too tired, while at the same time I feel slightly uncomfortable that I have turned down an invitation. It's always the same: if I say yes, I end up thinking that I would rather have stayed home, because I rarely enjoy myself with Emelie's friends, and if I say no I feel as if I'm being boring.

Baudelaire writes about loneliness, I underline almost every word. A feeling of being condemned to eternal loneliness, and yet a burning appetite for life. Would he have gone along to the student bar in Norrköping? That could never be enough for someone with a burning appetite for life, but he might have thought it was better than nothing.

I have started to go down to the harbor in the evenings, following the Motala River, which runs not far from my apartment, walking along the quayside in the direction of the sea. I rarely see anyone, perhaps the occasional dog walker or someone hurrying to catch the last bus.

In the inner harbor the floodlights are perched high on their triangular towers, casting a harsh, ghostly light over sheds and quays, corrugated iron, pallets, the enormous wooden cable reels. You can sit on the reels when they are not sodden with rain, looking at the town from the outside, the way the seamen experience it when they arrive, it is not an impressive sight, but it still carries the warm glow of civilization, the promise of people and terra firma and open bars.

Farther out lies the Pampus terminal. I don't know why it is called that, but I have always assumed it is because ships from the pampas dock there, ships from the other side of the world, from almost the very edge of the Atlantic Ocean, in my mind I see Argentina, vast plains, blue mountains. The harbor is at its deepest there, built for transoceanic vessels, I love that word, transoceanic, I picture white ships sailing across the open sea, the sun glittering on the waves, herring gulls close to the land, and then, far away from the shore, an albatross. These are ships that will recognize this inlet off an inlet off an inlet as the backwater it is, a nowhere town churning out bales of paper that are loaded into deep holds down below to become newspapers all over the world, *The Financial Times* and *Die Zeit* and *El País*, this is where they begin, in a sodden town that smells of sulfur, a town that mariners who have sailed the seven seas are happy to leave behind as soon as possible, happy to cast off, to set sail, to get away from here.

I have never had a plan for my life, and I have sometimes despised, sometimes envied those who have. The only thing I am really good at is writing. It is a compulsion within me, a need to put everything I think and feel into words, which is why I have always believed that writing is what I am meant to do. Perhaps that is naive. I could probably do something else, I found most subjects easy in school, because I am intelligent and have never needed to work all that hard. To be honest, I am lazy. That became obvious in my first term at university when I failed my first exam, I hadn't known I was expected to do any more than learn facts. I had gone all the way through high school without really learning the skill of abstract thought. It came as something of a shock, and a whole new area of life suddenly opened up to me. I had never experienced that kind of conversation at home, and I just didn't understand how everyone else could simply take it in stride, how everyone else in my class, who had also come straight from high school, could master the skill with such ease. I am still unsure of myself when it comes to things which are too abstract: philosophy, for example, which fascinates and frightens me at the same time, like a beautiful, exotic animal which I prefer to contemplate from a distance.

Perhaps I ought to become a teacher or a librarian, surely not everyone who follows those career paths can feel passionate about them, they have simply chosen a route and followed it through, that is how people live: they make a choice and stick to it, whether it is a matter of education and training or a job or a partner. I have never been able to do that. I always think that I have an uncompromising attitude to life in that respect, an attitude that makes things difficult for me, but which I cannot talk myself out of. I have the same attitude about everything: people, clothes, literature.

When I took a writing course and we discussed literature, I could never really understand the enthusiasm the others had for certain authors, particularly young Swedish writers. Some people talked about them as if they were geniuses. I usually found their writing somewhat self-conscious and insincere, although I had difficulty explaining my opinion. Most of the time I didn't even bother trying to explain, I just sat there quietly so that I wouldn't seem odd, like someone who didn't get it, or who had poor taste, although in fact I thought it was the others who didn't get it and had poor taste.

I had recently read Dostoevsky's *Notes from Underground* and Thomas Mann's *Death in Venice*, and I had just started *The Magic Mountain*, I said that the first day when we went around the table introducing ourselves and the course tutor asked what I was reading at the moment. Everyone else was reading stuff that I found utterly banal – one girl said that her favorite writer was Astrid Lindgren – and during the break they chatted about a debate in one of the morning papers, about the limited role of women in both life and literature, and the way they talked about it made me realize that they really did regard themselves as limited. I found it hard to grasp what they meant, but I didn't dare say so, because I thought that would prove that I was unworthy to join in with these conversations. I couldn't understand what they thought was limiting them, and it seemed to me that they were discussing a nonexistent issue. Just write what you want to write, otherwise there is no point in writing, that was what I wanted to say, but I got the impression that they felt they were writing on behalf of someone else: the female sex, the female experience, that it was their job to address certain issues in their writing and that they were proud to accept this task, out of some strange sense of duty, and that they then felt affronted when their efforts were not sufficiently appreciated. I thought about Dostoevsky and the man from underground; I wished he had been part of my group. He would have been more fun to hang out with. Hard work, of course, but definitely more interesting than the rest of them.

At the same time, the fact that I was not interested in their debates made me feel like a traitor. I couldn't get away from the notion that all forms of sisterhood would mean lowering myself to an inferior level, that I would be forced to diminish myself to some extent, to dissemble, and I cannot dissemble. I couldn't say this to anyone, including the boys, because they might have seen it as a way of making myself stand out from the other girls, of selling out my sisters in order to appear more interesting. But that was not the case; I genuinely felt I had nothing in common with them or the things that interested them. As the man from underground said, "On the whole I was always alone."

I sometimes thought about the prerequisites for female solidarity, about why I always found it suffocating and claustrophobic, why I never felt comfortable with other women. In a way I envied those who did, it seemed so pleasant, so reassuring: to be able to relax in a sense of community, to know that there was always someone there to provide support, someone to talk things through with, even though at the same time there appeared to be a template for the topics you could bring up. I still feel the same way with Emelie: she is irritated when I say something she perceives as unfavorable toward other women, she cannot deal with anything that deviates from the way she believes I should want to behave — for example the idea that I might want to go to bed with an older, married man. If I had been let down by an older married man, there would have been a template for the situation, for the constructs to which I had fallen victim, the mantra of oppression and the balance of power, patterns of destructive behavior. The sisterhood demanded that I renounce myself. I wondered whether other women felt the same, if they accepted it, like entering into a relationship with a calculation in the back of your mind that you are going to have to make certain compromises, but that the result—security, whichever form it may take—will make it worthwhile.

It often occurred to me that it seemed simpler to be a man. Not that I have ever wanted to be a man, quite the reverse; ever since I was a child I have been fascinated by everything to do with women, with the stereotypes of femininity, makeup and perfume, high-heeled shoes. I could spend hours planning what the wardrobe I hoped I would one day be able to afford would look like, which items of clothing it would contain, what fabrics—silk, cashmere, totally out of reach for me on an income that came from a student loan or casual work paid by the hour in the hospital cafeteria, but in a well-to-do future I would be the most elegant woman of all, and the most feminine.

Femininity was another topic I found difficult to discuss with other women; I somehow felt it wasn't entirely acceptable to embrace it as I wished to do, that it required a kind of metacognition, an ability to recognize the highly charged aspect of stereotypical femininity and its destructive potential, which to me was the idea that everything men routinely regarded as sexy was in fact objectionable and should not be given to them, for example the shaved pubes and thongs that the men's mags had taught them to want. Once that realization had been taken on board it was possible to move on, to look at stereotypical femininity with a theoretical distance, since the whole thing was a construct and a drama, in which after detailed study and careful consideration I had decided to play the female lead. "There's an idea behind it," I often heard people say when they were trying to define something good, whether it was a piece of art or an item of lingerie, but that was a lie; it had to have the *right* idea behind it. Being attractive to men is never the right idea.

Emelie felt that way, even though she had never put it into words, but I could tell from the way she dressed: smartly and expensively for a student, because her parents gave her an allowance each month. She bought good-quality clothes and always looked well groomed, unlike a lot of the other girls in her class who never wore makeup, and whose wardrobe consisted of ill-fitting clothes, shapeless jeans, hoodies, and backpacks. But there was something wonderful about Emelie's whole appearance, something well scrubbed and nonthreatening which, I had realized, made her incredibly appealing to the boys in the student bar. I knew that she would never try to look sexy for them. Sexy was forbidden. The student town of Norrköping was a chaste environment, in spite of the fact that people seemed to sleep with one another at the drop of a hat, in spite of the fact that we were a generation who had always been encouraged to go for whatever we wanted, but still hardly anyone ever talked about what was sexy. Perhaps the whole Zeitgeist was chaste, at least that was the impression I got from Emelie and her friends, who were the only people I met apart from my work colleagues. Self-aware students who did everything they could to distance themselves from working-class girls, even though they were doomed to buy their clothes in the same stores as these girls for financial and geographical reasons. At a party earlier in the fall I had got into a conversation about underwear. Two of Emelie's friends had practically tied themselves in knots trying to express their loathing for G-strings, such a vulgar item of clothing, while at the same time making every effort not to condemn those who wore them. In the end they agreed that anyone wearing a G-string just looked amusing, not sexy. "Amusing!" they shouted, triumphant in the knowledge that they had found the key to expressing their enlightened point of view without criticizing anyone else.

Femininity was an intricate network of rules with a minimal amount of leeway, where everything was unspoken into the bargain. I often caught myself wondering whether everyone else had been given instructions that I had missed, or if the confidence with which they seemed to proceed was the result of a lifetime of close female friendship, if this had a salutary effect on all those involved, if it had made them into perfect examples of modern women who had an awareness of everything, from their essential view of the world to their preferences in contemporary literature and insights into women's fashion.

Anyway, that's how I often felt: that everyone else was the same, while I was dramatically different. It was a self-obsessed view. It's hardly surprising that I like Dostoevsky's man from underground, I would sometimes think with a smile, and then I would feel a sense of relief: I am conscious of my own frailty, I am not crazy, perhaps I have a slight narcissistic tendency, but then so do all writers, perhaps that's not a bad thing.

He is wearing a wedding ring, I note when he finally visits the cafeteria. The name badge on his white coat says CARL MALMBERG, SENIOR CONSULTANT. He has short dark hair with a hint of gray at the temples. He looks athletic, with broad shoulders and a lightly tanned face. Presumably he's into sports in his free time, perhaps he plays tennis, isn't that what men like him do? Or perhaps he has gotten his tan somewhere abroad, I expect he and his wife have a house in Spain, Italy, France, they go there as soon as they have some time off.

"I don't suppose you have any arak to go with this?" Carl Malmberg's colleague says, smiling at me as he helps himself to a large bowl of pea soup. Pancakes are included, but there is no room on his tray, he will have to come back for them.

Carl Malmberg laughs and looks at me, I smile at him. His colleague is not the first to joke about arak to accompany the pea soup.

"I don't think pea soup will ever taste as good as it did when we were in the military," his colleague goes on. He is slightly overweight and is not wearing a name badge, his cheeks are red, as if he has been running. He suddenly realizes that he may have been tactless.

"Your soup is very good too, of course," he adds quickly.

"I didn't make it," I say, to indicate that I realize that the pea soup we serve here isn't particularly good, and that I can distinguish good pea soup from bad, just as they can, even though I don't actually like pea soup. "I just serve it up."

Both of them smile at me as they hand over their bright yellow lunch coupons, then they go over to a table by the window where two other doctors have already moved on to their pancakes.

Siv sends me to the utility room. She has fully recovered and is back at work. She likes to order the casual staff around, but it doesn't bother me at all. I have always liked clear instructions, and I prefer to have plenty to do so that I keep busy, I have never seen the point in standing around at work if there's no opportunity to do something meaningful instead – if I could go somewhere quiet to read a book I might do that, but I think hanging around chatting with other members of staff is just exhausting, I'd rather do the cleaning.

The piles of trays and plates look distinctly unsteady, I change over to empty racks and start to run the plates through the dishwasher. If you leave them out for too long, the pea soup dries to a hard crust and they have to be washed several times. It is warm and damp in the utility room, a particular smell from floors that never dry properly, of drains where leftover food is never properly rinsed away, steam from the dishwasher that makes my hair go frizzy. I am wiping up the sticky residue of pea soup from the floor next to the garbage when Carl Malmberg and his colleagues return their trays to the hatch, I think I must look disgusting, or at least totally unremarkable, a girl wiping up pea soup in a utility room. Then I remember the cream-colored bra that shimmers through my blouse if I push my breasts forward, so I straighten up, give the doctors a little smile.

"That was very tasty," Carl Malmberg's colleague says politely.

"Great – I'll tell the kitchen," I say. I try to adopt a perfectly balanced tone of voice which is meant to make clear that I don't really care, because I don't really care about this job, but that since I am here, I take pride in doing my job as well as possible, in behaving correctly toward the customers, being polite and a lot pleasanter than the sour-faced old miseries who have been wiping up pea soup in here for twenty years, maybe thirty. And I am wearing a sexy bra that just shows through my blouse.

Carl Malmberg looks at me, but he doesn't say a word.

At first this town was allowed to decline, and then, when the factories in the center had fallen silent and the workers had been relocated to the electronics company in its suburban bunkers, they decided to revive the heart of the town for others, not the workers: for the children of the middle class from all over the country who come here to study at the university, taking courses in media and communications in fresh, newly renovated former industrial premises where my maternal grandmother spent her entire working life sitting at a loom. The water that drove turbines and machinery flowed around the red brick and yellow plaster, the river was thick with salmon right in the middle of the town. No smoke rises from the chimneys these days, people come here to study instead. Just a few years ago the trend was to move away.

Emelie stayed, she has lived in the same two-room apartment on Södra promenaden ever since we were in high school. She is having a party before going out tonight, just as she did when we were at school. I have washed my clothes in the sink. My dress smells of peach detergent and it isn't quite dry yet, I've blasted it with my hair dryer but the seams are still a little damp. It's black so you can't tell, and the temperature is still above freezing outside.

She seems to have invited everyone in her class. She greets me with a kiss on the cheek, then goes off to talk to someone else, leaving me to open my bottle of wine in the empty kitchen, find myself a glass. Loud music that I don't recognize is playing in the living room, and people I don't recognize are dancing in the way that students dance when they are not quite drunk enough, slightly stiff and clumsy, with gestures to indicate that they are in fact dancing with an ironic take on dancing. When they've had a bit more to drink maybe they will have the courage to dance properly. I don't like dancing. A boy sitting on the sofa nods to me as I sit down beside him, then continues talking to a girl with bangs. I take my cell out of my purse, the time is 10:28, no messages. The girl gets up and goes into the hallway, the boy stands up and follows her. On the whole I am always alone. I sip my wine. I am tired, I should have stayed at home. My calves are aching.

"How's it going?" Emelie asks, draping herself over the armrest of the sofa with a cigarette in her hand, even though I know she doesn't usually like people smoking indoors.

"Okay, I suppose."

"Did you speak to Niklas?"

"Not really."

"He's nice, isn't he?"

"I didn't speak to him."

Emelie doesn't look pleased, she takes a swig from her can of beer and gets up.

"We'll probably be leaving in an hour or so."

The student bar is crowded and some band I've never heard of has just finished playing, the wine has made me feel a bit drunk. I am in a strange mood, sometimes I think the situation is unbearable and repugnant, then I think that perhaps this evening is a metaphor for my life: in my drunken state I think this is a perfectly reasonable comparison, that in fact it is my life that is either unbearable or repugnant, depending on how you look at it, but what kind of life is it if it is at best unbearable? The thought makes me sad. Emelie tries to drag me onto the dance floor even though she knows I don't want to dance, I get annoyed with her, I am tired, I suddenly feel like I can't stand any longer, I look for an empty seat but I don't see one. I lean against the bar and when the bartender asks what I want I order another glass of wine and immediately realize that I don't want to drink it, it tastes rough in my mouth, my feet are killing me. I don't know anyone here, I don't want to know anyone here, I fetch my coat and go home.

It rains and rains, the town is sinking. It is built on waterlogged ground. If you study photographs of the central station, you can see that there was a flight of steps leading up to the entrance a hundred years ago, now it is at ground level. The entire building has sunk, and the whole town will do the same. This is the old seabed, a barely concealed bog, mud and sediment, slime and clay beneath the streets and squares. When the trams go rattling by you can feel the ground shake. Soon there will be an accident, something will collapse, floating down the river on a layer of slime, a tram will plunge into the marshy ground beneath the cobbles, a disaster, a tangled inferno of metal and mud.

It is the weekend in Norrköping and I ought to do something but I don't know what, I might as well have offered to work. The rate for working unsociable hours in the main kitchen on weekends is good, I could have done seven till four on both Saturday and Sunday, washed the containers that had been used for the weekend's puddings, fruit-flavored soups, and fruit purees and creamy desserts that all have a cloying, synthetic taste, thick with starch, the containers are so difficult to get clean if they have been allowed to dry out. I could have gone to the antiquarian bookshop with the extra money and bought the edition of *The Magic Mountain* that I have looked at several times already, two volumes from the late 1950s in different shades of green, they would look lovely in my bookcase.

Carl Malmberg would stand in front of it, take out the first volume, and say that this is a really good book, a major achievement by one of the greatest authors of our time. "I know," I would say. "It's brilliant." He would be impressed by the fact that I have read it, he would never have guessed. He would sit down in my red armchair with the book in his hand, distractedly leafing through it as he takes a sip of his wine. He has brought a bottle with him, something I have never tried before because it is expensive, over a hundred kronor. He is wearing a shirt and jacket, he is very stylish. I am sitting on the sofa in a new black dress which is both classic and flattering, my body looks voluptuous in a tasteful way, like an expensive gift wrapped in beautiful paper. My apartment is clean and tidy. Carl Malmberg glances around the room, his eyes settle on me.

"You're not the way I had imagined at all," he says.

"What had you imagined?" I say.

Carl Malmberg gives a little smile.

"Don't take this the wrong way, but... you do work in the cafeteria."

"Oh no," I say. "That's just something I happen to be doing at the moment."

"So what are you really going to do?" Carl Malmberg says, taking another sip of wine. He is holding the glass in a firm grip, he is looking right into my eyes, genuinely interested in what I intend to do with my life. His expression is both considerate and challenging.

"I'm going to write a novel," I say. No, I am embarrassed by my own fantasy, it sounds painful. But that's what I want to do, so that's what I have to say. I *am* going to write a novel. Not just one, but several, I am going to be a writer. If I say it the right way, with conviction, not like someone who is just dreaming, but like someone who has really made up her mind, it will sound positive and ambitious. I am sure that Carl Malmberg likes people who are positive and ambitious, energetic, you can just tell. He likes it when things happen, he likes women who make sure things happen.

I go for a walk almost every evening. It is a compulsion, a restlessness within my soul that makes me go out after lying on my bed for hours with a book, when the town has grown dark and suddenly everything feels too constricted: my life, my apartment, my brain. I try to get away from my own thoughts. I listen to loud music as I walk, it frees me completely from the rest of the world, enclosed in a bubble.

When I reach the harbor I switch off the music, I have to be on guard down there, always prepared for something to happen, for the possibility that I may encounter someone who wants to do me harm: to rob me, rape me, kill me. It is a fear bordering on nausea, yet at the same time there is a hint of erotic tension, I remember feeling the same way as a child when I once watched a film that was too violent for me: simultaneously wanting to look and not look, to know and not know, to open myself to the horror and to cover my eyes.

These walks evoke a state that is almost an out-of-body experience, there is only me and the town and the smell of fall, the music and my own chain of consciousness, which is like a seismograph reacting to every shadow and scent and shift in the atmosphere. I wonder what kind of music writers usually listen to, what music all those who have written the books I love were listening to when they wrote them. Particularly the men who wrote about boys who traveled around Europe and met girls and got drunk and dreamed and read and talked; I want to write like that, not like a man, but like a woman who writes like a man. Other girls who think of themselves as intellectual have completely different ideals, which are often based on that feeling of inferiority and an anger directed toward it. I have never felt that way. I have thought that I would like to live the myth of the male artist: sitting in cafés and bars, smoking and drinking and discussing, traveling the world, reading all the books, seeing all the works of art, listening to all the music, feeling at home with the sense of not feeling at home, being a flâneur. There are no female flâneurs. I don't agree with that. I cannot accept a more boring existence simply because I am a woman, and because men have laid claim to everything that is enjoyable over the years.

A while ago I saw an advertisement for some kind of feminist cheerleading group on a notice board outside the university library. No doubt the concept was weighed down with theories explaining that feminist cheerleading does in fact have the potential to overthrow society, that's what happens when we get the idea that what men have promoted is always wrong, I think to myself: meaningless activities that we suddenly decide to take seriously. What a sad way to accept the limitations imposed by the female sex, while at the same time being convinced that we are doing the exact opposite. I would never be able to put up with filling my life with that kind of thing, or with reading what these supposedly feminist women read, at least not as far as I can see from what I have read, because it is regarded as typically male, self-obsessed, normative, I have always wondered why I have never met another woman who thinks the books I love are good, that the life they describe sounds cool, desirable.

I am a failure as a feminist woman. I am a failure as a perfectly ordinary woman as well, I am too clever – I said that to Emelie once when I was drunk, she got angry with me, really angry, she looked at me as if I was a traitor. I have always felt like a traitor. I am a traitor in every camp, because I don't really need other people. That is the greatest betrayal of the sisterhood, an awareness that you have no need for it.

I have searched in my books for others who are like me. Or for those who are the way I want to be: those who lay themselves open to life, who love and lose, who do not distance themselves from life with theories and ideologies. But things do not go well for them, these women writers, young, lyrical modernists who reveal so much about themselves, these nineties authors who write from the perspective of a completely unguarded love for one man. They never get the man they love. That makes me sad, because I feel as if they are writing about me, and that I am therefore doomed to failure. Is that the lesson we are supposed to learn from women who do not hide the fact that they want to please men – that they are doomed to failure? I want to please men too. It says in the feminist journals to which Emelie subscribes that it is disgusting to have rosebuds on our underwear, that we should cut them off because they symbolize little girls, that men who are turned on by rosebuds on underwear are basically pedophiles, it is somehow imprinted in them, being turned on by girls who are inferior to them. I have no doubt that most of the boys in the student bar like girls who are inferior to them, but it has nothing to do with rosebuds on their panties.

By chance I started listening to eighties music during the fall, electro-pop, the New Romantics, then Italo disco, overdubbed, synthetic, with banal lyrics that are somehow so honest and moving that I am captivated, and the sound of the synthesizer, always warm, like a dark night on the shores of the Mediterranean Sea, I have been there only once but the music captures the feeling perfectly: bittersweet. I listen to Italo disco as I walk along the avenues, through the linden leaves, I set one of the songs on repeat, it sounds almost military to begin with, but the song is naked, desperate: *You took my love, and left me helpless*, it makes me think about the books by women who loved and lost and ended up with nothing but a great sense of loneliness. I listen to it over and over again, I am almost hypnotized by it, I turn up the bass and lose myself in the music. It is the mixture of the superficial and the deeply felt that touches me, the melancholy and the joy of life, these are the very qualities that I value in other people. It is just that I have never met anyone with those qualities. Virtually nothing is honest, I think. If you are looking for honesty, then you had better be prepared to be alone.

He isn't there on Monday, it is raining on Monday. Siv and Magdalena chat about what they did during the weekend, about their families and relatives in the suburbs of Norrköping where houses and apartment blocks sprawl in endless, identical developments. They talk about a dog show, about Rottweilers and how they ought to be put down, they talk about TV shows I haven't seen.

I am often quiet at work, perhaps they think I am shy, and sometimes I really do feel that way, but mostly I am quiet because I find it difficult to join in with the conversation. It is not because I think I am above the topics they discuss, I like talking about ordinary things, but there is something about the situation that feels odd. To them I am someone who has been to college, unlike them, and that creates a distance. The fact that I am interested in reading and writing creates yet more distance — they seem to regard such activities as a punishment, the kind of thing they did in school and have been happy to avoid ever since, and I understand that, it's not that I believe everyone should be interested in reading and writing, but it does create a distance. Another problem is that I don't have a love life that I am willing to share with them, no boyfriend to talk about, no dates to report back on, that is a conscious choice on my part, I have no wish to confide in them. As a result an imbalance arises when they confide in me, which they sometimes do, but they usually confide in each other when we are all sitting around the table at break time and I just listen, like a silent witness, without giving them anything of myself in return.

He isn't there on Tuesday, it is raining on Tuesday too. I meet up with Emelie for coffee in the evening, there is a boy I can't place sitting at her table. Emelie seems proud to have him there.

"This is Niklas – you two know each other, don't you?" she says with a big smile, I realize he is the boy from her party, the one who was sitting on the sofa and walked away without speaking to me.

"We met at the party," I say.

He nods, says a reserved hello. He has a 1960s haircut which is simultaneously attractive and unreal, as if someone has dumped a hairpiece from another decade on top of his head, but he manages to carry it off because he is very good-looking, with well-defined features, he probably plays in a band, Emelie likes guys who play in a band.

"So how are you?" Emelie says.

"Fine."

"Have you been working today?"

"Yes."

"Where do you work?" Niklas asks.

"At the hospital... in the cafeteria."

Niklas looks disgusted for a second before he manages a slightly strained smile. He has very white teeth.

"Emelie and I are studying together," he says.

I nod. On the table between them is a pile of books by French philosophers on photography and cinema. Emelie is drinking her coffee out of a tall glass, she makes a slurping noise as she sucks up the very last drops through a straw, she looks happy, her cheeks are glowing.

"Do you want to come out with us tonight?" she asks.

"Where are you going?"

"Just to the student bar, but we're all meeting up at Niklas's place first. It would be awesome if you came. Wouldn't it be awesome?"

She looks encouragingly at Niklas, who nods. "Awesome," he confirms.

He lives in a two-room apartment on Östra promenaden. Perhaps the people who live on the avenues are meant for one another, I think as I walk up the stairs in the beautifully decorated stairwell, I admire the paintings on the ceiling, run my finger over the smooth surface of the dark wood paneling. Niklas has furnished his turn-of-the-century apartment, which is protected from the threat of demolition, with pieces from the sixties, expensive kitchen chairs and ceiling lights, it is a long way from the usual student bedsit, full of junk from flea markets and garage sales. Emelie says she loves his apartment, I mumble that it's great. She leaves me in the kitchen to open my bottle of wine.

"Hi," says a girl sitting in the dark at the kitchen table, I return her greeting.

"You're not in our class," she states.

"No. Is this some kind of class party?"

She shrugs. "I don't know. I thought it was, but now you're here." She smiles. "I'm Alex."

The way she pronounces her name sounds exotic, Russian perhaps, although to be honest I have no idea, I just think it sounds exciting. As I move closer and look at her in the glow of the candles on the table, it seems to me that she looks Russian too, or French perhaps, there is something about the way she holds herself; she looks self-assured. Beautiful, but most of all self-assured, with dark hair and a wide, friendly mouth.

"Who do you know?" she asks.

"Emelie."

She nods. "I know everyone. I have to see them every day at the university, and in the evenings I have to party with them."

I laugh. "Don't you like them?"

She shrugs again. "It wouldn't be very nice of me to sit here criticizing them to someone I don't even know," she says with a smile and a challenging look.

"Right."

"So we'd better hurry up and get to know one another so that I can start badmouthing them."

I laugh, she laughs too, her mouth seems incredibly wide, it takes up half her face in a way that I find captivating, I can't stop looking at her. I am still laughing when Emelie comes back into the kitchen wanting to know what we are laughing at.

It's not just because I am drunk that I find Alex fascinating, but in my intoxicated state it seems to me that she is verging on unreal: her appearance, the way she acts. I wouldn't expect someone like her to exist in Norrköping, then I tell her what I'm thinking and she laughs and says that's because she's from Linköping, then we both laugh and pretend to argue about which town is best. It is a completely meaningless discussion, the kind you only have with someone you don't really know because you have no idea what else to talk about, you just know you want to talk to them, and I drink in every word she says even on such a banal topic, it's like love at first sight, the kind of discussion that only feels meaningful if the person you are talking to means something to you.

We sit side by side at the counter in the student bar everyone always goes to after every student party. I ask her why this is the case and she considers the question as if it were a vital issue, she comes up with the theory that students only want to hang out with other students because they think that the world they inhabit is the most important of all worlds, and cannot imagine lowering themselves to hang out with perfectly ordinary people who have perfectly ordinary jobs.

"I'm one of them," I say, realizing that the wine has made me dramatic in a way that will be a source of embarrassment in the morning. "I'm a perfectly ordinary person."

Alex locks her eyes onto mine.

"You're not ordinary," she says, and I knew that was what she was going to say, perhaps I set a trap for her and she willingly walked into it, and I feel pleased that she has done exactly what I wanted her to do.

"Nor are you," I say.

"I know."

We are in silent agreement that we have paid each other the finest compliment it is possible to receive from anyone in this town, and Alex waves to the bartender, who as usual is a student who doesn't look entirely comfortable in his role.

"Two glasses of champagne, please!" Alex calls out.

The bartender looks confused. "I don't even know if we have champagne," he says in a broad Östergötland accent.

"Maybe you could check?" Alex says, and the bartender nods and disappears into a storeroom, and Alex and I look at one another and neither of us needs to say that we ought to be somewhere else, that this dump is beneath our dignity, we should be sitting in a bar in Paris or Berlin, and there too we would be the most elegant customers in the place.

"We've got sparkling wine?" the bartender says, holding up a bottle.

"That will have to do," Alex replies.

When the bartender opens the bottle and the cork shoots up to the ceiling with a pop that is heard above the music, and everyone turns around and looks as he pours the foaming wine into two champagne glasses, it really does feel as if we are not ordinary, not among the students or those who are not students or anyone else in this town, it feels as if together we can make life a little closer to the way we both want it to be.

He isn't there on Wednesday, it has stopped raining. It's a long time since I've seen him. His colleague has been in, cheerfully commenting on the well-spiced tandoori chicken that is the dish of the day. In the utility room the spices turn the pools of water red, making them difficult to distinguish from the red mold that spreads where the dampness never goes away, in the nooks and crannies both inside and around the huge dishwasher. It is unhygienic and must be dealt with by following strict instructions from the manager of the main kitchen. I am liberal in my use of an antibacterial spray until the entire utility room has a sharp, acrid smell. Disinfected.

It is windy outside when I finish work, the damp chill penetrates my clothes, I press myself right into the corner of the bus shelter. The tips of my fingers are still wrinkled from washing up, I have given up wearing gloves because I think they smell so horrible, rubbery and medicinal, but it means my nails always look ugly, I hate not being able to wear nail polish at work. It could chip and fall into the food or onto the dishes, it would be unhygienic – a perfectly reasonable rule, but it still gets on my nerves. Even if they would be ruined every afternoon when I do the dishes, perhaps I should at least have nice nails during the lunchtime rush.

It will be fifteen minutes before the bus comes, I must have just missed one. I am just about to head back to the hospital foyer to read my Baudelaire book while I'm waiting when I see Carl Malmberg coming toward me. I recognize him as he enters the revolving doors, he is tall, taller than most of the other doctors, he strides past the low concrete planters with their withered asters, his scarf fluttering in the wind. As he passes the bus shelter I catch his eye and give him a little smile.

"Hi," I say.

He stops.

"Hi yourself," he says, sounding slightly surprised but friendly, as if I seem familiar but he can't quite place me.

He is wearing dark blue jeans and a dark jacket, he looks very stylish. I realize I have never seen him in anything but his white hospital coat. Perhaps he is thinking the same about me, I speculate, as I notice him glance at my boots, then up my legs.

"Finished for the day?" he says.

"Yes."

He smiles at me. "I didn't have time for lunch today. It was chicken, wasn't it?"

"That's right."

Now we are both nodding.

"The chicken is usually pretty good," he says.

He doesn't seem to want to end the conversation. I can almost see him searching for something to talk about, ransacking his brain, his eyes darting from side to side. Eventually they settle on the electronic display inside the shelter.

"Which bus are you catching?" he asks.

His smile is warm, he doesn't look anywhere near as stern as he sometimes does in the cafeteria, he has cute laughter lines around his eyes.

"The one-sixteen," I say.

"Twelve minutes... ," he says.

"I just missed one."

"Do you live in town?" he asks.

Vapor emerges from his mouth as he speaks, it must have got colder, below freezing after several mild, rainy weeks. His checked scarf is made of wool, in muted colors, it's smart, all his clothes are smart.

"Yes, down by the theater."

"In that case… I mean it's on my way home, so I can give you a ride if you like."

I knew he was going to ask me, I think. Maybe not just like this, but I knew something was going to happen. Something is going to happen now, that's very clear. At last something is going to happen.

"Are you sure it's no trouble?"

I am testing him. It won't be any trouble.

"No, no." He smiles. "It's no trouble at all."

"Well, in that case… ," I say, smiling back at him. We are entering into an agreement, I think. Nothing will be the same from now on. Whatever happens, something will have happened.

"I'm over here," he says, waving toward the western end of the parking lot, the area closest to Emergency. He strides away and I can only just keep up, he slows down a little.

"You've been on duty quite a lot lately," he remarks.

"I guess I have."

"Are you full time now?"

"No, I'm employed by the hour."

He nods. "Are you hoping for a full-time post?"

"No… no way."

Carl Malmberg glances at me, smiling again.

"How come?"

"I don't really want to work there at all."

I think about my fantasy, imagining him back in my apartment, and I have to smile to myself. He drives a Volvo, the latest model, he has kids of course, that hadn't occurred to me before. The car is a deep, dark blue, it is a beautiful color, it sparkles like a starry sky. He takes out his keys and deactivates the alarm, then he opens the passenger door for me.

"Madame."

It is a very clean car, there is no child seat, no discarded toys or candy wrappers or any other trace of children. There is an English paperback carelessly tossed on the back seat, nothing else.

Carl Malmberg gets in and takes off his gloves. He has beautiful hands, well cared for, I think they are probably very sensitive, then I push away the thought, how stupid, where did I read that, in a story in some old magazine perhaps, doctors and their sensitive hands. I feel myself blushing slightly. He looks at me.

"Down by the theater – is that Bråddgatan?"

"No, Vattengränden... it cuts across."

"I know it."

He starts the car, it sounds muted. Then he makes a few adjustments to the heating before backing out of his parking space with an expression of great concentration on his face.

We don't say anything for a little while. I think I ought to ask him something, something about his job would be logical since he's asked about mine, but everything that passes through my mind sounds childish. I'm sure he's glancing at me, I sneak a glance at him when he's looking the other way. He's handsome, he looks younger than when he's in the cafeteria, perhaps it's his name badge with the title SENIOR CONSULTANT that makes him seem older. In the hospital he's always busy, stressed, but now he's more relaxed, he drums his fingers on the steering wheel, smiles at me.

"Are you studying at the same time?"

He looks at me, I meet his gaze.

"Not at the moment," I say. "I'm going to start in the fall."

"For a qualification in the restaurant industry?"

I give a little laugh.

"No," I say. "This is just a temporary job. I'm not planning on a career in catering."

He nods. "So what do you want to do?"

"I'm going to apply for an advanced course in literature."

It feels as if I am talking to an elderly relative.

"Cool," he says, sounding slightly distracted. He doesn't seem surprised, and he's definitely not impressed as I had hoped he would be, there is no indication that he wouldn't have expected me to say such a thing, he just keeps nodding. Perhaps he comes from a world where everyone has taken advanced courses in college, where it's nothing special, nothing to be impressed by, particularly when it comes to a useless subject like literature.

Perhaps he's boring, I think. Perhaps he plays golf, perhaps that's his only hobby, perhaps he shares it with his wife. They go to their villa in Spain which is right by a golf course, they play golf all day every day, he's not interested in culture or politics, he's interested in golf. On the way to Spain he randomly picks up a couple of English crime novels at the airport, does a little reading on the plane, on the beach, never finishes a book. Suddenly it feels odd, sitting beside him. The spontaneous connection I thought we would have just isn't there. We sit in silence. He drives along the avenue, turns off, stops outside my door.

"There you go," he says. "That was a bit quicker than the bus anyway."

"Absolutely," I say. "It's very kind of you. Thanks."

"Are you working tomorrow?" he asks.

"Yes."

"In that case I might see you."

I get out of the car, he gives me a little wave as I close the door and I wave back, I feel confused. Maybe he regretted offering me a lift the second he spoke, realized it was a strange thing to do. Or it might have been some kind of test, and I've failed. Maybe I shouldn't have said yes. Maybe he thinks I'm boring.

Sometimes the smell of sulfur blows in from the paper factory and settles over the town, it penetrates everything. In the areas where no effort has been made to renovate and bring in a new freshness, the town is decaying; back alleys stinking of urine, parking lots clumsily hidden behind wooden fencing covered in graffiti, dilapidated old buildings down by the harbor, the Virginia creeper that has wrapped them in a blanket of dark green. I think about the earwigs that live there in the cool darkness, finding cracks and holes around windows and doors, they always manage to get inside, just like the smell of sulfur.

The trees lining the avenues are beautiful for a short while, glowing yellow. It is like a cathedral, with the dark, damp trunks forming tall columns supporting a ceiling of gold mosaic, shimmering high above Östra promenaden, while Södra promenaden is like a long golden hall, but with a lower ceiling this time, it is like a gilded grotto, the linden trees are younger and haven't yet grown as tall. Then they drop their leaves in a final exhalation before winter, and the leaves look beautiful on the ground for a moment before pedestrians and cyclists and dogs trample them to a slushy mess, the sweet smell of decay, of earth and dampness. And they gather in the gutters, in the tramlines, the claw marks leading down to the harbor. All roads lead down to the harbor, where the waters of Strömmen begin their journey to the sea, away from this backwater, this inlet off an inlet off an inlet, this appendix to the Baltic Sea.

Some years ago a large vessel was anchored out in the bay for several months, a ship from Russia carrying workers who were laying a cable on the seabed. They were welders, laboring away under the water, I liked to picture the scene: like a fireworks display in slow motion, sparks slowly flaring into life only to disappear immediately, fading away in the dark water. At night the whole ship was lit up, it had strings of lights around the railings and the funnel, it glittered like a deserted funfair on the black surface of the sea, the extended reflections forming a halo of light around the outline of the ship.

People said that the Russian welders came ashore at night. They rarely ventured into town, but kept to the areas on either side of the inlet; the number of break-ins allegedly went up, everyone blamed the welders. All the bicycles that were stolen were going to be transported to Russia and sold, apparently.

In a bar in a small community on the northern side of the inlet, the welders met two local girls, one of them went to my high school, the rumor spread like wildfire that Monday morning: the girls had gone back to the ship with the welders in the little motorboat they used to get ashore, they had gone to bed with them, all of them, all those Russian men who spent their days underwater. The numbers increased as the rumor was passed on: it was five men to start with, then ten, twenty.

I imagined that it had taken place up on deck, naked bodies beneath the glimmering lights on a dark, mild, late summer's night, perhaps the slow bobbing of a dying swell, carried into the inlet from the sea beyond, the sound of passion drifting ashore. People were upset, disgusted, I thought it was a beautiful image.

It was a long time since I had enjoyed meeting up with Emelie. It hadn't really bothered me very much until now, the endless rounds of coffee drinking had seemed a little distant but still pleasant, reassuring in its predictability, as if we were an old married couple. When we first got to know one another in high school, I already knew that in a way we weren't really compatible, and that we had just become friends in order to avoid having lunch with someone even more boring.

I would like to be able to tell her about Carl, tell her exactly how I feel: that I am attracted, *really* attracted to a married man, that it's exciting, that it could be an adventure. That it feels like fun. But as soon as I mention him I notice she has to make a real effort to be on my side. Perhaps she actually wants to tell me off, to shout and get angry, bawl me out on behalf of all the women whose men cheat on them, blame me for a whole history full of men who left their partners for other women, women with low morals who ruin things for everyone else. I think that's how people would regard someone like me:

a woman who wants to sleep with a married man could also be a woman who wants to sleep with your boyfriend. Not to be trusted, that's what I am. That is how Emelie is beginning to regard me.

At the same time, I don't know why I need her approval. She obviously doesn't need mine, she's always doing stuff I would never do. She goes to the feminist cheerleading group, and not only does she think it's fun, she finds it rewarding and energizing. What she is doing shows loyalty toward women. I am disloyal.

I don't know why I think everything I do needs the approval of other women. It feels like I will be brought before a women's tribunal to justify every decision I make, while at the same time I have no interest whatsoever in the approval of other women. I sometimes wonder if I'm a misogynist, but I've never heard of a female misogynist, and in any case I don't really hate women, I just find it difficult to empathize with them, and I admire some women: perfectly ordinary women who struggle to make ends meet, bringing up children and running a home under difficult circumstances, or women in history who were pioneers in traditionally male fields, doctors, lawyers, all those ambitious women who did the kind of thing I would never have the courage or the energy to take on a hundred years later, two hundred even. And I am fascinated by other women simply because they are beautiful, some have faces and bodies that are like works of art, I can lose myself in them, gaze at them for an eternity, until it becomes inappropriate. It is an aesthetic admiration, possibly erotic to a certain extent, I have always been drawn to beauty.

I also hate men who hate women, and I hate women who hate men, to be honest – no, you're right, hate *is* a strong word, it's more that I despise them.

"Not much meets with your approval, does it?" Emelie once said to me when I was talking about some people who were annoying me at a party, her tone was acid but she said it with a smile, and afterward I thought it was a perceptive comment, even amusing and perfectly correct: not much meets with my approval.

I decide to tell her about Carl Malmberg anyway, tell her he offered me a lift and I accepted. Emelie stares at me.

"Seriously?" she says.

"Yes."

"Did he come on to you?"

"Not at all."

That's not a lie, he didn't come on to me. Perhaps offering me a lift constitutes coming on to me, it probably does, but nothing else happened. I tell her the whole thing felt a bit weird, I didn't really know what to say to him, I ended up feeling confused more than anything.

"Just watch out," she says.

"What?"

"Watch out for married men."

I laugh. "What do you know about married men?"

She looks offended, sips her coffee.

"Enough," she says. "I know you need to watch out."

In a way she is right, of course. Boring, but right. I realize it's not a good idea to sleep with a married man, not to mention falling in love with a married man, which is a risk that must be taken into account, but I also think it's a risk he has to take into account, that in some ways it would be worse for him if that's how things turned out: he would have to leave his wife if he fell so deeply in love with me that he could no longer stand his other life, while I would be the beautiful younger woman for whom men leave their wives.

"Alex was asking about you," Emelie says instead of continuing the discussion about Carl.

"Was she?"

"She said she thought you were cool."

"Did she? Is that exactly what she said?"

I ignore Emelie's expression, which is suspicious and annoyed at the same time, I really want to know what Alex said about me.

"I think so," Emelie says patiently. "We're working on a group project together, so she came over yesterday."

"She came over to your place?" I can hear a hint of jealousy in my voice, which makes Emelie's expression change from irritation to satisfaction.

"She's pretty elusive," she says.

"What do you mean, elusive?"

She shrugs.

"Kind of hard to get a handle on."

"I like that," I say.

"I'm sure."

I don't know what kind of smile she is wearing now, it is friendly yet at the same time slightly supercilious, as if she thinks that Alex is elusive, but so am I, and that she knew we would get along. It makes me feel proud, because it means she thinks I am like Alex, and there is no one in this whole town that I would rather be like.

It is raining on Thursday, he's not there. I am usually free on Fridays, because the cafeteria is quiet on Fridays and they don't need to bring in any extra staff, and a feeling of indolence pervades the afternoon, almost a sense of warmth and coziness. This is proof of man's ability to adapt to anything, I think, the facility to survive anywhere, the fact that I have started to see a warm coziness in this ugly cafeteria in this ugly hospital. Then I think perhaps it's actually proof that I feel at home here, and on some level that doesn't match the image of who I want to be. This makes me simultaneously happy and sad: I have no plans to continue doing this kind of job, everything I have done over the past few years has been with the aim of getting out. But in my darkest hours I have thought that this kind of work is what I am genetically destined to do, programmed by generation after generation of workers. In that same fundamental way I sometimes feel out of place in university corridors and seminars, afraid of opening my mouth in case I give myself away, exposing the fact that I don't fit, that I've hustled my way in. Writing saves me from those thoughts, because if I really was meant for a life in a catering kitchen, I wouldn't have that impulse, I tell myself, that need to put all my ideas into words. Some time ago I printed out a picture of Harry Martinson and stuck it on the door of my refrigerator and kept it there for ages. It's the one where he's so handsome, young, leaning forward, with lovely thick hair, wearing an expression that is both sensitive and challenging, as if he was looking at me, just me, and saying, *If I could do it, you can do it.*

The cleaning is soon dealt with and we can relax at the table by the window with a cup of coffee and a chocolate cookie, we haven't bothered putting any money into the kitty. Siv and Magdalena are gossiping about someone I don't know, I am only half listening as I watch dusk fall over the parking lot. Then we say our goodbyes, they take the elevator down to the windowless underground corridors to attend the weekly meeting in the main kitchen, I don't have to go. I get changed in the empty changing room, lock up the cafeteria, and set the alarm. The whole hospital has a sleepy feeling today, noises are somehow muted, it's dark outside, the rain is hammering on the windows.

The rain reaches almost right into the bus shelter. In spite of the darkness I see him from a long way off this time too, coming through the big revolving door that is like a carousel of light. I have time to watch him as he hunches his shoulders against the weather and hurries through the parking lot. Then he catches sight of me.

"Hi there," he says in just the same way as before when he reaches the bus shelter. He is wearing the same clothes as last time too, jeans, coat, scarf. His hair is a little ruffled from the wind.

"Hi," I say.

"I didn't get around to lunch today either," he says, sounding almost embarrassed. I smile. He smiles back.

"Did you have any lunch?"

"I usually buy a sandwich from the kiosk."

He shakes his head as if to indicate that he should know better, and that the sandwiches from the kiosk are horrible. The conversation already feels more intimate than last time in spite of the fact that we've hardly said anything, there's something about the atmosphere, it's more relaxed today. He steps inside the bus shelter to get out of the rain, and suddenly he is standing very close to me. He looks up at the display.

"Four minutes until the bus comes?"

I nod. "Yes."

"I enjoyed your company the other day."

His expression is friendly, he really does know how to look kind, I've never noticed that in the cafeteria.

"Me too," I say.

He smiles, tilts his head in the direction of his car.

"Let's go."

We talk more this time, both of us. He seems to be in a better mood, he tells me about working as a kitchen hand when he was in medical school. Not in a hospital but in top restaurants in Stockholm, and as he speaks I realize that his voice has no trace of the clumsy dialect everyone speaks around here. His pronunciation is neutral, clear, pleasant. Now and again he had to help out in the bar, just doing simple tasks. He once mixed a gin and tonic for Bryan Ferry, he tells me; he looks delighted when it's clear I enjoy the story.

"We used to get really good tips sometimes," he says."I don't suppose you get much in the way of tips?"

"Well no – almost everyone pays with their lunch voucher."

He laughs, his laugh is short and loud, it sounds honest. I think that he probably doesn't laugh at things out of politeness, but I also think he laughs easily, it's a sympathetic laugh. Uncompromising in a sympathetic way.

When we pull up outside my apartment, he keeps talking.

"Where do you live?" he asks.

I point to my window, facing onto the street, the lower section covered in baking parchment.

"On the ground floor?"

"Yes."

"Do you like living here?"

"It's okay. It can get a bit noisy outside on the weekends, that's all."

He nods, looking at my window.

"Well, thanks for the ride," I say to break the silence, even though I don't really want to go.

He has unbuttoned his coat, he's wearing a shirt and a woolen sweater underneath. When I was growing up I didn't know a single man who wore a dress shirt for work. I can hardly take my eyes off it. He looks at me and smiles.

"Are you working tomorrow?"

"No. I'm not sure when I'll be in again."

I don't know if it's my imagination or if he really does look disappointed. There is a hint of what must be his cologne in the car, it is spicy but soft, like cinnamon, it smells warm. I would like to be close to him, I suddenly think, breathe in that scent. I undo my seat belt, wanting him to say something that will keep me sitting beside him for a while longer, but he doesn't say anything. He waves to me as I close the car door, I wave back, hearing Emelie's voice in my head. *Watch out for married men. What do you know about married men? Enough. I know you need to watch out.*

There is a party at the School of Art on Saturday. Niklas has been invited by someone he knows and he has invited Emelie, who has invited me. When I arrive at Emelie's she immediately puts a glass of wine in my hand and sits me down on her bed while she carefully tries on a selection of dresses. It's obvious that she's already a little tipsy, and that she's nervous, and even though she's asking me which dress looks best, I realize that she's actually asking which dress I think Niklas will like best.

He meets us on the way to the party, gives her a hug, and greets me politely but with a certain amount of reserve. I am well aware that he doesn't like me. It really shouldn't bother me because I don't like him either, but I allow myself to be provoked by the way he looks at me, by the fact that he always makes me feel cheap. I'm sure it's not his intention, he's very well brought up, he's attractive in the way that the children of rich, attractive people are, in a completely self-evident way, his whole bearing speaks of yachts and tennis lessons and studying abroad, it's part of his body: a mixture of good health and worldliness. I am uncomfortable in his company, because he seems uncomfortable in mine, he has the ability to make me feel judged. And cheap, from a purely concrete point of view, because he has a much better apartment and more expensive clothes, a supercilious accent and a supercilious way of coming out with everything he has picked up about French philosophers at the university, but also in a more subtle way, as if there is something about me that bothers him.

I have always known that there is something vulgar about me, something I cannot hide. It is embedded within me from generations gone by, it is not going to disappear because of a couple of college courses and a few college parties, I have felt it all my life, even as a child: the aura around some of my classmates was different, more solid somehow. Even though I have never been anything other than perfectly wholesome, there were certain individuals who somehow always managed to be even more wholesome, who always had more practical clothes, surrounded themselves with possessions that even as a child I realized were different. Perhaps at the time I didn't realize that they were more expensive, they appealed to me because they were more rustic, gave a more solid impression. Bicycles that seemed to be of higher quality, notepads that seemed to demand neat handwriting and good spelling, with their encouragingly tasteful design. Raincoats and boots that weren't the cheapest because their wearer would soon grow out of them, but were well made and practical, handed down from older siblings, yet they were not unfashionable because they had never been fashionable in the first place. Beautiful, practical cases for musical instruments – they had lessons after school, of course; no cavities in their teeth, and then their hair: simple styles that were easy to look after, and their names, even the names of these children were solid and simple: Elin and Emma and Klara and Sara, carrying with them the promise of good behavior and eventually good grades, good future prospects, good career opportunities, unshakable self-confidence.

Since then I have disliked such uptight perfection out of a sheer sense of self-preservation, while envying it at the same time, and despising myself for doing so. Sometimes I have thought that my whole being is vulgar, that I am made up of components that are a little too much, each and every one: my body is slightly too voluptuous, my mouth slightly too fleshy, nothing about me is toned down or cute, I like high heels and lots of makeup and tight clothes. It's as if something about my posture, or my aura, is more tangibly sexual than almost any of the girls I have met at Emelie's parties, at the university, in the student bar, and guys like Niklas find this provocative, or disgusting, perhaps even frightening, it's as if there is something about me they can't handle. I have noticed that it is guys like him, the educated, modern guys, those who are most aware that it is unacceptable to divide women into madonnas or whores — they are the ones who make sure they have a girlfriend who could never be mistaken for the latter.

Perhaps the men who are interested in me are the kind who are aware of that vulgarity within me but are not frightened by it, men who are interested anyway, or perhaps for that very reason. Perhaps they are men who are vulgar themselves. It makes me wonder about Carl Malmberg.

Norrköping School of Art is in one of the former industrial areas, right next to the Museum of Labor, which also used to be a factory — that was where my grandmother worked.

The School of Art is new, it was established just a few years ago. It's really supposed to be a School of Sculpture, and there are rolls of chicken wire and great big sausages of clay wrapped in plastic everywhere, there is plaster dust on the floor, but most of the students are working on completely different art forms: video, performance. People come here from all over the country to study. A short distance away on the other side of the Museum of Labor and the Motala River is the statue of Moa Martinson, who also worked at the looms, she gives an impression of no-nonsense sturdiness, it seems to me that she is looking right through the buildings, keeping a stern eye on the art students and thinking that they ought to get a haircut and find themselves a job. I also think that she is looking at me with a critical expression, she can see that I want to go to bed with her husband. Traitor, that is what she thinks of me.

First-year students' expressionistic creations made of chicken wire hang from the ceiling. Outside the walls of the school the water thunders past, hurling itself down a drop and landing in a cascade of foam before surging on through the town and out to sea. You stop noticing it after a while, the noise fades into the background but is ever present, you can feel it right through the building, a slight vibration. I'm sure the whole place will collapse one day, come crashing down into the water, and these priceless works of art will be lost forever. I can't help smiling to myself.

People around me are eating a vegetarian chili, there are paper plates everywhere and the smell of dampness and cheap tinned vegetables pervades the room, it reeks of student accommodation. On the tables there are candles on paper plates, you're allowed to smoke indoors, so I light up because I'm bored, I will go home when I've finished my cigarette. I can see Emelie and Niklas not far away, talking animatedly to each other, Emelie is gesticulating enthusiastically, it's obvious she's in love.

I am about to get up and leave when I see someone I recognize in the middle of a group of people by a door leading out onto a balcony. She notices me at the same time, waves, extricates herself from the group, all of whom appear to be dressed in black, makes her way over to me, gives me a hug.

"Great to see you," she says, her mouth close to my ear so that I can hear her above the music. "I wondered when we'd meet again."

"Did you?"

She smiles, her mouth, painted with dark red lipstick, is almost unnaturally large in her face.

"I said we ought to get to know one another, didn't I?" she says. "And I don't say things I don't mean. You have to come to the after-party."

It is a mild night, the air is almost warm, a late fall night when you can go out with your jacket open, it feels unreal. I am just tipsy enough. I am so self-aware that alcohol doesn't always affect me: even when I have drunk a great deal there are often moments when it is as if I am observing myself, evaluating what I say, realizing that I am babbling, coming out with things I haven't thought through, being ridiculous. "You're making a fool of yourself!" my brain says to a different part of itself, and that embarrasses me, makes me pull back. I very rarely feel the way I do tonight, as if a great calmness has descended over all my senses. I am not sleepy, my brain is sharp, but it feels comfortable, it has settled down and for once it is simply letting things happen, without raising any objections.

Alex wants us to drop by someone she knows who lives in the center of town. Someone else texts her the entry code, and soon we are standing inside a beautiful elevator with teak paneling and brass details and a soft, warm light, we are slowly moving upward. The party is in a big apartment on the top floor, there is a generous terrace and we stand side by side, smoking and gazing out over the town in the dark, warm evening.

I point toward the harbor, toward the orange lights that are visible even from this far away, the floodlights illuminating the empty quays.

"Sometimes I think I should get on a ship," I say. "Like Harry Martinson did. Fish up cables from the bottom of the Atlantic."

Alex looks at me, her eyes locking onto mine. Her eyes are magnetic, I think, which sounds perfectly reasonable in my current state.

"Stop it," she says.

"Stop what?" I say, partly irritated, partly curious because she is challenging me.

"Do something real instead," she says. "Write a book. Just sit down and write. Or do something you can write a book about. Don't keep wandering around and dreaming."

She passes me a bottle of sparkling wine that she has stolen from the host of the party, I don't know if it's a man or a woman. I take a few swigs but end up pouring too much in my mouth, it runs down my chin, down my throat and my chest. Alex laughs. Then she reaches out and traces the rivulet of wine with her finger, sticks her finger in her mouth and licks it.

When she notices that this makes me uncomfortable, she smiles with satisfaction.

"You're such an innocent," she says quietly.

"No I'm not," I protest.

"So what do you do that isn't innocent?" she says. Her expression is teasing. I feel my cheeks flush, possibly with embarrassment because she makes me feel childish, but also with pleasure because she seems to be interested in me, in what I do and ought to do.

"I have a lover," I say.

"What kind of lover?"

"A real lover. Not some guy I just sleep with, but a real... man. It's kind of like in a film, he's much older than me... and he's married."

Alex smiles, sizing me up. It's a smile that makes me think that I like her, and that I want to get to know her. That I should have met someone like her a long time ago.

A guy who looks as if he's still in high school suddenly staggers out onto the terrace, grabbing the balustrade next to Alex for support.

"You're interrupting," she says sharply.

"I live here, for fuck's sake," he replies.

We both laugh. He looks angry and confused, but Alex offers him his own wine until he cheers up and puts his arms around our shoulders, telling us we're the prettiest girls who've ever been in his apartment, and we laugh again and I think that at long last things are going to be different.

Then it is as if my brain gives me permission to think about Carl. At first it annoys me, the sense that yet again I need someone's blessing, which Alex has now given. But then my irritation is washed away by all the other thoughts, they are much stronger, surging forward as if a dam has been breached, like a river carrying me along. A weighty feeling of excitement settles in my body, wrapping my mind in cotton wool. I think about him when I am at work, when I am standing in front of the enormous dishwasher feeding in crate after crate of dirty dishes, when I am wiping down table after table in the cafeteria, when I am scrubbing and cleaning and drying the heated counters and the heated cabinets and the heated trolleys.

I imagine his hands on my body as I stand at the dishwasher, he is standing behind me, I close my eyes and think of his hands finding their way inside my clothes, how it will feel when they touch my skin for the first time. The smell of dampness in the utility room becomes a part of my fantasy, and eventually it is so intimately linked with him that it begins to feel erotic, until a sudden wave of excitement floods my body every time I walk into the room and smell the dampness and in the steam from the dishwasher I picture his hand on mine, on my thigh, I see him kissing me.

He is standing by the newspaper kiosk next to the main revolving door, I see him as soon as I start walking down the stairs. He catches sight of me before I get to the bottom, he watches me as I walk toward him. This makes me feel awkward, I don't know where to look, I am afraid of tripping. I should have put on some lipstick.

"Hi," he says when I reach him.

"Hi."

"What a day."

It is raining, it has been raining all afternoon, lashing against the cafeteria's big windows, drumming on the windowsills. Inside the main door the floor is wet and dirty, the parking lot outside almost seems to have dissolved in the pouring rain. The shrubs are almost bare now, just a few intensely red leaves still cling to the black branches, the water dripping and trickling from them.

"Actually, I don't mind as long as the temperature stays above freezing," I say.

He looks at me with curiosity, as if I have said something interesting. Then he turns and walks toward the door. I stay where I am because I don't know if he was waiting for me or someone else or if he was waiting at all, I don't know whether to follow him or not. After a couple of steps he turns around.

"Coming?"

"Oh, yes, I..."

"I saw you this morning," he says as he leads the way. "I happened to walk past the cafeteria, so I knew you were working today."

"It was kind of you to wait."

"My shift just finished, so I thought..."

The sentence dies away, he gives me a little smile. Today his car is parked right next to the projecting roof over the entrance, so we don't have to get wet. He deactivates the alarm and before he opens the passenger door he glances around to check if anyone has seen us. It is dark outside, although some light spills out onto the cars parked closest to the hospital, but in this weather there is no one around who is thinking about anything other than protecting themselves from the downpour.

We talk all the way home. This time I pluck up the courage to ask him some questions too, where he lives, where he's from. He was born in Stockholm, but lived in Uppsala for a long time.

"You don't have an accent," I say.

He smiles, seems delighted that I have noticed.

"You could be right. Neither do you."

"I've done my best to avoid it."

"Why's that?"

"Because I come from Norrköping."

He laughs this time, his short, loud laugh.

"I thought the accent sounded terrible when I first moved here," he says. "But I'm used to it now, and sometimes I think it can sound pretty cute."

I shake my head, smile. We have arrived at my apartment, I notice that I have forgotten to turn off the lamp in my window. Carl Malmberg notices it too.

"That looks real cozy," he says.

He's right, it does. It is dark outside, and the Vietnamese lantern gives off a soft, warm glow. He has switched off the engine, there is silence inside the car, the only sound is the rain hammering on the windshield. He clears his throat.

"It would be nice to see your apartment sometime," he says.

He looks at me, his gaze steady.

Suddenly I feel as if I am holding my destiny in my hands, weighing yes against no, that at this precise moment I have the chance to change things. We are making a pact right now, I think. This is when I ask him if he would like to come in and he says yes and nothing will ever be the same again. What happens from now on cannot be undone.

"Would you like to come in?" I say.

He glances down at his watch, nods. I know he is going to say yes.

"Great," he says.

We get out of the car, he locks it, and we dash through the rain to the apartment block and, inside, over to my door. He stands behind me as I open up, I can feel his eyes on my back. I have rarely felt more present in the moment, I register everything – the grain of the wooden door frame, his scent, the key sticking slightly in the lock before it turns – while at the same time I am acting entirely on instinct.

He follows me in, closes the door behind him. Then he turns around and looks at me. His presence fills the entire hallway, the entire apartment. Then he moves forward, places one hand behind my head, draws me toward him and kisses me. It is a firm kiss, I put my arms around his neck and press my body close to his, he kisses me harder, I feel dizzy, I cling to him. He takes a deep breath.

"Jesus," he murmurs.

He pushes me away, his expression almost accusing, before he kisses me again, opens my jacket and slips his hands around my waist, but soon they find their way downward, he holds me tight, presses me close.

He smells just as good as I expected. I lay my face against his neck and inhale the spicy scent of cinnamon, then he lets go of me to shrug off his coat, slide my jacket down over my shoulders, he kicks off his shoes before we move like one single clumsy entity toward my bed, we fall down with him on top of me, his body is warm and heavy, he slides his hand under my sweater and places it on my stomach, determinedly moving it upward.

It is still raining. I hear the rain in the distance somehow, hammering on the window as he slowly and deliberately makes love to me, or screws me, I don't really know what to call it: it is completely different from the way things have been with guys my own age. There is nothing of their impatience, the sense that they feel as if they have gained access to something that will soon be taken away from them, so they have to be as quick as possible, exploit it to the max. They are like bulimics, I think, binge lovers, with their own pleasure uppermost in their minds.

Carl Malmberg talks to me, tells me I am beautiful, asks me to touch myself, and I do as he says in a state of arousal that is nothing like anything I have experienced before. His body enfolds me completely when he wraps his arms around me, I am lost in his embrace, he tells me to come and I obey.

After that the town seems different to me. It is full of possibilities, it is as though my whole existence has grown bigger, deepened, acquired both a greater darkness and a greater light. To think that things can be this way, that you can have a secret like a dark strand, a pulsating bass line beneath everyday life. It feels adult. I don't know what else to call it, yet at the same time it is something I couldn't have imagined in the past. When I was younger I could never have imagined that life as an adult would be like this, that other adults around me – parents, relatives, teachers – could have parts of their lives that weren't open to everyone, that were something different from outward appearances, from the normal routine, work and leisure.

Secrets were what people had in films and on TV, I would never have believed that films and TV portrayed such things because that was reality. Perhaps it is thanks to my secure upbringing that I believe life consists of only one layer, I think, the layer I am part of, the layer that is suitable for children.

Suddenly I feel like a part of something bigger, a tacit agreement, a club for people who have realized that one aspect of life can be about something they don't talk about. That nothing is what it seems to be. I think that maybe it's natural, just as our taste buds demand bigger kicks as we get older, we suddenly crave sourness and bitterness and saltiness after the mild, nondescript tastes of childhood. Over and over again I wonder why I have never done something like this before.

I learn the rules of being a mistress so quickly that I feel I must have a particular aptitude for this role. Perhaps I have, perhaps a mistress is what I am meant to be. I toy with the idea of writing a guide for mistresses, containing practical advice. I can't give any emotional advice yet, I will have to add that chapter at a later stage.

I learn never to adjust the passenger seat in his car. His wife is shorter than me, and the seat is as far forward as it will go, it would be more comfortable for me to push it back slightly, but I never do, in case I forget to readjust it and she starts wondering who has been in his car.

I wear very little perfume. On the days when she might want to use his car soon after I have got out, I am not allowed in the car at all, because the smell of me would linger. He has informed me that even my hair has its own scent of shampoo and conditioner and hairspray, he sounds pleased but there is warning in his tone. And my skin, even if I don't wear any perfume at all, carries the scent of my shower gel. Sometimes he takes my arm and pushes up my sleeve and sniffs the inside of my forearm because he thinks I smell so good.

I never wear lipstick or lip gloss. I avoid pressing my face against him when he is dressed, because of the risk of getting makeup on his shirt.

I switch my cell to silent as soon as I am with him, in case she calls and my phone might ring while they are talking and she would wonder who he is with.

I check that there are none of my long, dark hairs on his sweater or jacket or coat before he leaves me. His wife is blond, I have seen her hairs in the car. No doubt she has lovely hair. No doubt she is beautiful. I have asked a few questions about her, even though I'm not sure I want to know the answers. I have a picture of her in my mind, maybe it would be better if I didn't. I have read that horror films are more effective if we don't see the monster, it is more frightening if it exists only in our heads, because nothing is as horrible as the things we can imagine. A wife that I could only imagine would have been worse. But then he told me she is nine years younger than him, it's his second marriage, she works in corporate law, and I thought I shouldn't have asked. It all sounds so attractive. It makes me wonder why he wants a mistress, especially why he wants someone like me, who spends her day in an ugly hospital uniform clearing away leftover food.

I picture his wife as incredibly beautiful and successful, cool and elegant with her perfectly styled blond hair and smart clothes that are both formal and businesslike, no doubt she is entirely professional in the way that has always frightened me. I have never felt comfortable around people who are very goal-oriented. I'm sure she is well respected at work and a good mother to their two children and has an active social life, she is interested in sports and cooking, they are both very sociable and often invite friends around, they are an attractive and popular couple with a lovely home, like in an American film, airbrushed to perfection.

That's how I imagine it all. Sheer envy over her perfect life means that sometimes I think she deserves to be betrayed. You can't have everything. Her life would still be better than most people's, even if her husband is cheating on her. It almost seems fair.

Then I am ashamed of myself.

Then I wonder why I am ashamed of myself.

Then I see one of her blond hairs on his coat and it slices through me like a knife, stabs my heart like a cold, sharp icicle, and I think that because she wishes me ill, I wish her ill, it's only fair.

Dostoevsky wrote that only beauty can save us, I used to think about that in my writing class, where I concluded that there was an unspoken suspicion of anything that was beautiful, from the fact that none of the girls at college seemed to wear makeup, and there was a fear of beautiful writing, beautiful scenes, beautiful language. It was beauty that got me interested in art and literature from the start, if they hadn't been beautiful I wouldn't have wanted to know about them. My need for culture began as a basis for dreams, ideas about how life could be in the very best-case scenario, a kind of springboard to greater heights. Are you really so spoiled? That's what I sometimes used to wonder about my classmates. Do you have such an excess of beauty that you need to slum it a little bit, embrace what is ugly? I pictured their family dinners and vacations, beautiful apartments and views, made up conversations in my head. It was a kind of bourgeois cliché which probably didn't match up with the reality at all, no doubt most of them didn't come from the privileged upper class, but from the perfectly ordinary provincial middle class, with parents who were teachers and social workers and dental hygienists, but even then, I thought, there were books and summer cottages and people who could play the piano. And some of those sitting around the table in my writing class actually did have parents who were doctors and lawyers, I found it more difficult to get involved in their work, I just thought, how hard can life be when there's always a safety net? When there's always a parent who can pay the rent if things really go wrong, when you never have to feel like someone has pulled the rug from under your feet when you lose your job or your apartment, and you suddenly find yourself in the middle of nothing.

That sense of security must do something to people. That's how I regard the cultivated well-to-do upper-middle class: so secure in all the fundamentals of life that they are able to devote themselves to other things, get involved in relationships, in their spiritual life, see a therapist, fulfill their potential, argue over family dinners. I think it's a kind of first-world problem, but perhaps the need for problems is a constant: if you don't have problems, then you create them.

"Have you ever had a real job?" That's what I want to ask everyone I meet, even if I know that almost all of them have had a real job, but a few days here and there in market research or a summer job as a care assistant doesn't count, the only thing that counts is when it's a matter of life and death, the jobs you do because there is no alternative, because they're the only jobs you can get, and if you didn't take them you wouldn't be able to pay your rent, and there's no one you can ask for help. The jobs that are the alternative to the abyss.

The only thing that counts is to have known the abyss.

But I don't want to study social realism either. I don't really like depictions of the working class at all, they are always depressing, people are alcoholics and it's all ugliness and wretchedness and misery. I can't relate to that either. I grew up with food on the table and an underlying sense of security, but with a lack of culture, a feeling that the world is small, that certain things are meant for other kinds of people. It annoys me when best-selling books about the working class describe social misery, it doesn't have to be that way. There is a working class who live decent lives on very few resources, they work and do the right thing, they are clean and healthy and well brought up, but submissive when they have to deal with anyone who can be regarded as being in authority: teachers, doctors, official bodies, even restaurant staff on those few occasions when they eat out. They would never complain about a diagnosis or a grade or an unsatisfactory main course, they don't want to be any trouble. No books are written about them, perhaps because their lives are without drama. I ought to write about them, but I don't want to. And yet I miss them, both in the arts and in the general consciousness, and it irritates me that it is impossible to refer to the working class without evoking a fleeting response of disgust or pity in those who immediately think of domestic violence and misery and tramp stamps.

Sometimes I don't know what I like. Nothing is good enough. It's not a particularly attractive quality. I can hear Emelie's voice inside my head: *Not much meets with your approval, does it?* She's right. That's why I think that art must raise itself above the ordinary, that it must resist demands for representation and realism, that it must be bigger than that.

Sometimes something is so beautiful that it feels like a religious experience. I have never had a religious experience, but I'm guessing that's how it would feel. It can happen when I am reading a novel or a poem that completely swallows me up, or when I see a really, really good painting. It's difficult to explain, it's like a dizzy feeling, a sense that this particular piece of art puts its finger on something that is on a totally different plane, a higher plane, to my mind a truer plane. As if it has come close to an absolute truth.

That too makes me self-absorbed, believing that I alone have the ability to see which works in the history of art are the most true—because that is what I think, that I can recognize the best art, that I have a particular sensitivity which enables me to tell when something is true. This conviction often depresses me, all I have to do is read a page in the culture section of the newspaper, find out what is regarded as good in contemporary circles: all that miserable ugliness, that stupidity which is held up as important social criticism, allegedly showing the power and potential of culture.

My favorite is early Renaissance art. There is a purity in those paintings that is unlike anything else. They are not perfect, the perspective is skewed, but there is something else about them, a quality that flashes across the centuries like a bolt of lightning and enters my soul. All the pictures feature a God I don't even believe in, but it doesn't matter: when the angel comes to Mary with a lily in his hand and tells her that she will conceive and bring forth a son, I feel as if I am there in the room, feeling the seriousness of the moment beneath the chalky white arches.

That's where you can talk about the power and potential of art, I think. But perhaps I am like a person who is convinced that she sees ghosts: far too preoccupied with something bordering on madness. None of my contemporaries seems to have any interest in quality or beauty, and I think that those who are like me, who seek for something greater, more beautiful and more true, look elsewhere rather than to art and literature, they turn to other contexts where they can find the same experience:

to religion, or nature, where I have had the same dizzying sensation when faced with a particular view or landscape, an impression of beauty so strong and immediate that I believe it is an important part of the meaning of life.

And that's how it is when I have sex with Carl. It is the same sensation, that my life is growing and shrinking at the same time, that everything that exists and is of any value is restricted to that moment, to our bodies, to the smell of him. When I feel him above me I am transported to a different state, something completely new, I am weightless, as if an anchor that was holding me fast, locking down my consciousness, has been removed: it strikes me that I have never felt less like myself, so much in my body rather than my soul, or perhaps it is the other way around: I have never felt so much in my soul rather than my body, it is as if I am in some kind of primeval state, I have never felt so much like a child, like an unborn fetus: vegetating, enclosed, primal, yet at the same time I have never felt so grown up as when I meet his gaze and he grips my wrist and presses his lips to mine.

I am in the kitchen behind the cafeteria preparing the salad buffet when my cell phone buzzes. I have been given the responsibility of the salad buffet on the days when I am working, and I like having a job which is mine and mine alone. I want it to be perfect, although I have to work within the available parameters, which are incredibly boring. The porter brings down fresh ingredients from the central kitchen, several containers every morning: huge crates of grated carrot, lettuce, sliced cucumber, winter-pale and rock-hard tomatoes. Canned and pickled vegetables are available in big tins in the larder. I don't understand how anybody can come up with such an uninteresting salad buffet, I have tried to explain that nobody really likes canned vegetables, and that nobody eats lettuce these days, I can't even remember when I last saw lettuce served anywhere. We could add a little fresh fruit, I suggest, perhaps put together a few combinations and pickles of our own, but no one seems interested, which annoys me, but at the same time I think maybe they're right, what do I know about salad, or how to run a cafeteria, I'm only a student, as far as the kitchen staff are concerned I could just as easily be a creature from outer space.

So I work within the limitations, I serve up the pickled vegetables. The cans are opened with a gigantic opener fixed to one of the worktops, and the smell of vinegar pervades the entire kitchen. I have tipped out pickled gherkins and black olives and carrot and cauliflower and silverskin onions and beets when I hear my cell phone vibrating on the draining board. *1 message received*. It is from Carl, he has started texting me during the day. His messages are usually about sex, what he's going to do to me. Just seeing his name on the display turns me on. "Thinking about you. What are you doing?" it says. I reply, the phone buzzes again in seconds. "Can you come up here?" I tell him I have to work, he sends me the number of an examination room, a floor and a department. "Tell them you have to go and buy something from the pharmacy," he writes. "Hurry up."

It is only ten o'clock, there is no rush with the salad buffet. At any moment Siv and Magdalena will go and sit by the window with their coffee. It doesn't matter if I miss my break. I throw the big empty cans in the garbage, tuck my phone in the pocket of my blouse. Siv is just making fresh coffee.

"I need to go and get something from the pharmacy," I say. "I won't be long."

She merely nods, looking crossly at the coffee machine, which is old and has a thermostat that doesn't work properly.

The corridor is deserted. It doesn't take me long to get to the department where Carl is. The room is more difficult to find, I end up in a little staff room with chairs made of birch wood, prints on the walls. Nearly all the art I have seen in the hospital is ugly and depressing, produced in the late 1980s, it consists almost entirely of prints in gaudy colors. There is a woman in charge of cultural activities within the hospital, she organizes guided tours where she talks about the art collection. I wonder if she actually likes this stuff, or if she just turns up and tries to do her job as well as possible within the prevailing parameters, as I do with the salad buffet.

Eventually I find the right examination room. I feel a little unsure of myself as I stand there, my knock sounds feeble in the empty corridor. Carl opens the door immediately. I smile at him but he doesn't smile back. He is wearing his white coat and his name badge, CARL MALMBERG, SENIOR CONSULTANT, and his expression is serious, he closes the door behind me, presses a button so that the sign will light up, indicating that the room is occupied. There is an overwhelming smell of disinfectant, and something else: plastic, rubber, and the dryness of the paper covering the bed in one corner. On a small cart I see jars containing cotton swabs, compresses, bandages, the desk over by the wall is empty. There is a calendar hanging on the wall.

"How's it going?" I say.

He doesn't answer. The curtains are white with a pale, abstract pattern, the sun is shining today, a faint haze hangs in the air, it is almost like spring. Like a day when you screw up your eyes to look at the sun and see herring gulls drifting against a pale blue sky, you hear their screams and know that you are close to the open sea. Carl pulls out the desk chair, sits down. He nods over at the bed, indicating that I should sit down on it, so I do. The paper rustles and crumples around me, it is rough. Carl clears his throat.

"Thank you for coming," he says. His tone is formal.

"I can't stay very — " I begin, he interrupts me.

"Unbutton your blouse, please."

"Sorry?"

"Your blouse. Unbutton your blouse, please."

It is not a request, even if it is formulated that way; it is an instruction. Or an order. There are fluorescent tubes on the ceiling, the light is cold and flat, I will freeze if I get undressed. Nevertheless I start to undo my blouse, the buttons are large and awkward, imitation mother-of-pearl. Carl nods at me, at my breasts, I realize this means he wants me to unfasten my bra too, so I do. He gets up, comes and stands in front of me, looks straight at me.

"Good," he says.

His voice sounds different, detached, it hardly even sounds like him, if I closed my eyes I would think someone else was talking to me, someone with a deeper, monotone voice.

He leans forward, slips his hand beneath my blouse and bra. Then he cups my breast, I hear him take a deep breath.

"Good," he murmurs as he weighs my breast in his hand. "That feels good. They're lovely."

He opens my blouse and gazes at my breasts, nods.

"And your pants," he says, taking a couple of steps back. "Unbutton your pants as well, please."

I shift off the bed, the paper rustles. I unbutton my white pants. Carl clears his throat again.

"I think it's best if you take them off," he says.

I do as he says, I bend down and unfasten the indoor shoes I wear for work, kick them off, and remove my pants. Then I sit down again, feeling a little silly. Carl nods, moves to stand in front of me once more. He places one hand on my thigh, moving it gently in circles. It is warm, it feels nice against my skin, I close my eyes, I am aware of his scent, and immediately all the clinical smells in the room disappear. He moves his hand between my legs, slowly getting closer to my panties, then he pushes the fabric aside with his other hand, touches me. I keep my eyes closed.

"Good," I hear him say in that same distant tone. "Excellent. What a good girl you are."

He continues touching me, his fingers moving faster but still gently, my breathing quickens.

"*Ssh,*" he whispers. "You have to keep absolutely quiet."

He keeps on stroking me, my breathing getting faster and faster, then suddenly he stops, steps back. He reaches for a paper towel and hands it to me.

"Good," he says yet again as he sits down at the desk. "Everything seems to be in order."

He watches me as I wipe between my legs with the paper towel, I pull on my pants and shoes. My cheeks are burning with arousal and something I can't place, embarrassment perhaps, or discomfiture. Even though it was nice. I would like him to keep going, but he just sits there, looking at me.

"So..." I say.

At last he smiles, a very small smile.

"So," he says. "I'll be in touch before too long. It's probably best if you get back to work now."

I swallow, nod. I leave him sitting at the desk, go back to the cafeteria, start decanting salad dressing.

I tell Alex about it when we are drinking wine in the bar of a hotel that has just opened in the town center. It is perhaps the ultimate proof of Norrköping's transformation, the fact that a hotel that wants to be hip and modern has opened, a hotel that wants to attract a clientele that appreciates good design. The very idea that someone interested in design would have traveled to Norrköping a few years ago was bizarre, but now there is clearly a client base for such a place, I try to imagine what kind of people might stay here: guest lecturers at the university, perhaps, guest musicians with the symphony orchestra, guest curators at the Museum of Art, visitors who are keen on culture, and perhaps the odd former Norrköping resident who has come back to attend a wedding or christening. They will say to one another, "Who would have thought there would be a hotel like this in Norrköping!" because that's exactly right. Who would have thought it? Alex and I are sitting side by side on a sofa in a corner, with a good view of the rest of the bar and the lobby. The wine costs twice as much as in the student bar, but there is no doubt it's worth it. I don't know why I haven't been to a place like this before, but maybe there wasn't one, and anyway I wouldn't have had anyone to go with.

Alex smiles at me over the rim of her glass.

"But he didn't do anything else to you?"

"No. He just stroked me. And then he kept on texting me, all afternoon and all evening, telling me what he was going to do to me."

"Have you ever been to his place?"

"No. I don't know if I'd want to; I think it would feel weird."

"Do you know what his wife looks like?"

"No, and I don't want to know. I do know she's blond and she's younger than him. I bet she's gorgeous."

"She might have aged badly," Alex says, grinning with her wide mouth, I have to laugh, and even if it's much more likely that Carl's wife has aged extremely well, with good food and exercise and expensive skincare products, I really like Alex for saying that.

Carl and I quickly establish unspoken rules for our topics of conversation: I make it clear that I don't want to know anything about his home life, about what they do as a family, and when they go away for a weekend and I realize they're probably going to visit his in-laws, I don't ask any questions because it's so unpleasant, picturing him in a situation where he is chatting and hanging out with his wife's parents, who are naturally very fond of him, how could they be anything else, and the idea just seems grotesque, it almost makes me feel sick. I also realize there isn't much wrong with his marriage, no major crisis or impending divorce, it's just that he's bored with the whole thing, mainly because he doesn't feel desired, as far as I can tell.

There must be something wrong with a woman who lives with Carl and doesn't make him feel desired. How can you have a man like him in your home and not tell him every day that he's wonderful, that he's the most beautiful thing you've ever seen when he's falling asleep, that he's so hot you could just die when he walks in, smelling of fresh air and fall and the warm scent of cinnamon, with his checked scarf wound around his neck and his hair a little mussed up by the wind, that he's the sexiest guy you've ever seen when he steps out of the shower with just a towel around his waist, that gorgeous torso still tanned even though it's late November, that you can't stop looking at him, because he is like a work of art, like something you never thought you would get this close to. And when he gets into bed with me and I run my fingers along his arm, which is the most beautiful arm I have ever seen, I can see veins and muscles beneath soft skin, and I tell him exactly that, tell him I've never seen such a beautiful arm, and he looks at me in surprise. And I say surely he must know he has amazingly beautiful arms and he says no, because no one has ever told him that.

It's unbelievable. There must be something wrong with her. She has only herself to blame. It's such a waste, a man like Carl Malmberg being with a woman who doesn't appreciate him, it makes me angry just to think about it, it's like some kind of cosmic injustice which I am helping to put right.

In spite of the fact that I am so absorbed by him, by the relationship, the sex, the way he looks, his character, I also understand the mechanism behind the whole thing, I know that this is about an attraction based on a need for approval, on both our parts. Because it works both ways: I have never felt as desired as I do when I am with Carl, nothing has even come close to this. He can spend hours telling me what he likes about my body, the body I used to regard as little more than a vulgar container for my soul, it turns out he loves it, almost adores it. He thinks everything about it is perfect, he says surely I must realize that the first few times he saw me working in the cafeteria all he wanted to do was tear off my clothes and touch me. How could I possibly have known that? I felt disgusting in my ugly uniform, with a dishcloth in my hand and my face shiny with sweat from the heat and dampness of the utility room.

"It was obvious that you didn't really belong there," he says. "It was written all over you, you looked so elegant somehow, even though you were wearing the same uniform as everyone else, but I could see it in your eyes. There was intelligence there, I knew you were too intelligent to stay in that job for very long."

I drink in every single word. That's the best thing anyone has ever said to me. How have I gotten through life without someone who says things like that to me? I want to be the person he sees when he looks at me. I know I can be that person. Whatever happens, I have to make sure he doesn't see me as I see myself.

On one occasion he says he will understand if I want to see other guys, that of course he can't stop me, nor does he have the right to from a moral point of view, given his own situation, but the idea upsets him and he doesn't want to know anything about it. I nod and say okay, although I'm not seeing anyone else and have no desire to do so. And even though it's a reasonable thing for him to say, it makes me feel sad, because I'd really like to hear that he doesn't want me to see anyone else. I'd really like him to say that what he and I have is a little too wonderful for him to cope with the rest of his life; that his other life, the life I don't want to know anything about, seems intolerable now that he knows how things could be, that he can't go on like this, and that if I promise not to see anyone else, then he promises to leave his wife as soon as possible. But he doesn't say that.

Alex makes me tell her everything about Carl. At first I am embarrassed, but when she has plied me with enough wine, I notice that I enjoy talking about him. She listens attentively, as if my life were an exciting novel, and I love the feeling that gives me. She is also like a novel, or a film, bordering on overblown, but so skillfully balanced between the grand and the totally ordinary, the superficial and the profound that it just makes her more real. The depth I have encountered in most other people my age has almost always been contrived to some extent: predictable, based on a student's perception of profundity, political commitment that has always involved the same options, an interest in literature that has always been centered on the same books. In comparison with all this Alex comes across as unworldly, sometimes almost naive in her lack of guile, her lack of interest in seeming to be something she is not, while at other times she is smart and cunning, shameless in a way I have never encountered before. All her qualities are rooted in exactly the kind of honesty I have searched for, and that honesty pervades everything about her, including her apartment, which is odd in a way that fascinates me, yet at the same time it is not in the least ostentatious. I have been in enough student accommodation to know that the way most places are decorated makes the person who lives there appear to be anything but interesting. In Alex's apartment you have to pick your way through mismatched pieces of furniture, dusty, old-style potted plants on pedestals, tassels and fringes and crocheted mats. Persian rugs cover the floors in every room, so that the whole place is red and cozy, and all the sounds are muted. On top of a big dark armoire sits a stuffed barn owl, a male, glowing white, its huge dark eyes made of glass staring down at me, it looks ghostly. It was given to Alex by her mother, who inherited it from her mother.

She tells me that her mother is from Russia. She doesn't really say much about herself, but she's happy to talk about her mother, Elena from St. Petersburg, Alex is like her, she shows me pictures of Elena when she was young, and she looks like a 1970s version of Alex, the same dark eyes, the same wide, generous mouth. Elena lives in Linköping now, that's where Alex grew up. She mentions her father only in passing.

Alex is in the same class as Emelie but doesn't really hang out with her, she dismisses her fellow students as dull and boring.

"I think I want to sleep with my graphic design tutor," she tells me one evening.

"How exciting. What's stopping you?"

"He wears leather pants."

I burst out laughing.

"Have you ever slept with anyone who wears leather pants?" she wonders.

"I've never even known anyone who wears leather pants."

"I'm not sure whether he's a synth pop fan or whether he rides a motorcycle, and to be honest they're both as bad, particularly since he must be forty-five, but the worst-case scenario would be if he listens to synth pop *and* rides a motorbike."

"What's wrong with listening to synth pop?"

She waves her hand in the air as if she is trying to get rid of an unpleasant smell.

"There's something wrong with a middle-aged man who still dresses to match the music he listens to," she mutters, before taking a swig of her wine and looking at me with a satisfied smile. "But I think I'm going to have to try to sleep with him anyway."

I like everything about her, I like the fact that she laughs a lot and has big breasts, which makes her look voluptuous. None of the other girls I have met at the university look like her, they are pale and skinny, as the girls in humanities classes usually are. I realize it's unreasonable to assume that humanities students always look the same, not just in what they wear but in their body type, but I can't help it. Perhaps I am so self-obsessed that I like Alex mainly because she reminds me of myself. Or she reminds me of how I want to be. Carefree. What wouldn't I give to be carefree.

When I talk about Carl she asks for more details about what he does to me, what I let him do. I blush as I tell her, and she gives me that big smile and tells me I'm sweet, and that it all sounds very sexy. Talking to her about it feels sexy too, I like Alex's smile because it is hungry and inviting, not in terms of eroticism perhaps, but in terms of life, or adventure, something that is more exciting than my life has been so far, but on the other hand: maybe there is an element of eroticism too, so I smile back and make a little more effort so that she will keep on smiling in my company.

I manage to lift the lid of the drain underneath the dishwasher, it is full of little holes that let the water through but trap food waste, today it is covered with peas and diced carrots. Magdalena dropped a canteen of boiled vegetables on the floor, they've ended up in the drain filter along with solidified lumps of mashed potato. I think about Carl as I lift the lid with a hooked metal rod, I think about Carl as I tip the vegetables into the waste disposal unit, I think about Carl as I use the jet wash to sluice dried-up mashed potato off the inside of the dishwasher, the bottom is covered in a thin white film that also has to be rinsed away, there is a pile of salmon baking trays that someone rinsed in water that was too hot, which made the protein coagulate so now they have to go in the granule dishwasher where little hard bright blue plastic balls whisk them clean in an intense hailstorm, in the dampness and the dirt and the clatter of sticky trays I think about Carl. He always looks so clean. He always smells so clean, and it is infectious, that feeling of cleanliness, I become a different person when I am with him, within his smell. I become more like the person I want to be.

I feel lonely in the evenings, it starts at twilight. My heart reaches out toward the horizon like an empty bowl; fill me up, I think, fill me up with anything at all. I look out the window, see people walking past, men on their way home from work, heading for the bus or the train, going home to their families, they are dressed for winter, slightly stressed, any one of them would do, I think, I could open the window, stick my head out and ask one of them to come inside. Just hold me for a little while, you can touch me, do almost anything you like, as long as you hold me afterward.

There isn't a soul in sight when I go for my walks, they are all at home with their families. All the men are sitting on a sofa with a wife; they may not be in love with her anymore, but they still won't leave her. They are happy to cheat on her forever and a day, but they can't imagine leaving her. They prefer to stay in a relationship without honesty. That's what adults do, I think. Then I wonder about the wives. Are they happy? Do they suspect anything? I think about this as I walk from the harbor to the bus station, it's not very safe around here this time of night. This is the red light district, if such a thing exists nowadays.

I read in a book that female prostitutes are the modern city's equivalent of the male flâneur; they make the city their own at night in the same way, strolling past strangers and meeting their eyes. But while the flâneur merely thinks that he could have loved the person who has just walked by, the prostitute offers to do it for real, for a while at any rate. The book didn't say anything about female flâneurs. Women who walk the streets are whores. I've never seen one, but cars sometimes slow down alongside me, hoping I will turn out to be someone else. Perhaps I am someone else.

I would like to text Carl but I'm not allowed; I'm not allowed to contact him unless he contacts me first in case his wife sees it, he is with his wife tonight. He is at a parent-teacher conference, or maybe they've been to the movies, or they're sitting on the sofa drinking tea and watching a film right now, the whole family, like some glossy American Christmas card. I can't compete against someone who has given birth to his children, I think, I get angry with myself, angry with my own childish thoughts. I've been through it all, imagined us traveling somewhere, he takes me out into the world, to southern Europe, we can be seen out and about together, he can hold my hand and take me out to dinner and see other men glancing enviously at him because I am young and beautiful, perhaps they imagine us going home and making love, perhaps they think how lucky he is. But he doesn't want to be lucky, he wants his Christmas card family. Someone like me can never be a part of a life like that.

"I've bought you a present," Carl says.

He is holding out a bag from a lingerie chain, there is a package inside, a white box tied with a silk ribbon. It's very pretty.

"Wow—but why?" I say.

He gives a little smile.

"I guess it's a present for me, really," he says quietly. "You don't have to… but I think you'd look lovely."

I take out the box, pull the shiny ribbon to undo the bow, lift the lid. There is tissue paper inside in exactly the same shade of pink, and when I peek underneath there is even more pink: pink fabric, pink lace. It is a short camisole and a pair of panties, both made of the same almost sheer pink fabric, which feels a bit like nylon. They are kind of weird, they look childish and cheap at the same time, certainly not something I would have chosen for myself. Carl is looking at me, obviously waiting for a reaction.

"Very nice," I say.

"I think you'd look lovely in them," he says again.

"Do you want me to put them on now?" I ask, and he nods.

I take the box into the bathroom, get undressed, put on the pink lingerie. The fabric is stiff and slightly abrasive, the panties are very low cut, when I look in the mirror I can practically see right through them.

Carl gasps when I walk back into the living room. He is sitting in my red armchair, but immediately gets to his feet. I switch off the overhead light, it is embarrassing standing in front of him in my underwear in such a bright light.

"No, switch it back on," he says.

I switch the light back on. Carl moves to stand in front of me, very close, gazing at me.

"I knew they'd suit you," he says.

"Thanks," I mumble.

"Turn around."

I shake my head. "No…"

"Turn around," he says again, his tone is sharper this time. I do as he says even though I don't like feeling scrutinized, I think he's bound to notice that there's something wrong with me, that I am defective in some way, that he will realize this is a mistake, that I am ugly. Slowly I turn around, he nods.

Then he starts to undress. He unbuttons his shirt and takes it off, unzips his pants and steps out of them, removes his socks. He keeps his eyes on me the whole time, then he walks over to the bed, turns back the covers.

"Come here," he says.

I slip in next to him, he puts his arm around me, draws me close. I inhale his scent, nestle closer, gently kiss his chest, lay my cheek against it. I can hear his heart beating, I feel safe and secure, it is warm under the covers.

He caresses my hair.

"You're so lovely," he says.

His voice is soft and thick, he keeps on stroking my hair, allows his hand to slide downward, over my breasts, outside the camisole.

"You look so wonderful in these clothes," he says. "Beautiful."

He leans toward me, kisses me softly.

"You look like a little girl," he says. He looks at me searchingly. "Are you my little girl?"

I glance up at him. His expression is different, softer, almost pleading.

"Are you my little girl?" he says again, speaking more quietly this time, he is almost whispering.

I nod. "Yes," I mumble.

He moans, presses himself against my body. I can feel his hardness against my thigh. He kisses me again, my cheeks, my forehead, more passionately now.

"My little girl," he murmurs with his mouth close to my ear as his hand moves downward once more, over my breasts, my belly, my panties. Now I am the one who is moaning. Of course I am his little girl. I am whatever he wants me to be.

When I attempt to rationalize it to myself, I decide that I am doing it so that I will have something to write about. That I am exposing myself to life in the same way as those writers I admire, that I go along with everything he asks me to do because it might make a good story. Then I think that what makes them good writers is the fact that they don't lie, not to themselves or to anyone else: I'm actually doing it because it feels nice, because it's nicer than anything anyone else has ever done to me. I am doing it because I would do whatever he asked me to do.

Everything about him turns me on, but perhaps the most exciting thing is that he's older than me, that he's a real man, an adult. I read somewhere that men who have daughters are better than other men at undressing women, when I read it I thought it sounded sick and perverted, but it's true of Carl. He is usually eager to get my clothes off, but occasionally he deliberately undresses me very slowly, just to turn me on even more, but he always does it in a way that is both firm and tender, and he makes me feel totally safe.

He has ruined me. I will never be able to settle for lesser men, for incompetent men. With clumsy hands.

It is Wednesday but Carl and I can't see each other because it is his daughter's birthday. She is his eldest daughter from his first marriage, Sandra Malmberg, and she is twenty-four today. I am only a few years older, it's not that long since I turned twenty-four. I remember a birthday cake in the living room at my parents' house, a vase of lilacs, an envelope containing hundred-kronor notes.

Carl and the rest of his family are going out for dinner with Sandra, he has told me what usually happens: she is allowed to choose the restaurant, and they are going to one of the few really good places in Norrköping. I can picture the scene, a big table reserved in Carl's name, the family arriving in a big, well-dressed group. Sandra has been eating out since she was little, and knows how to behave in a restaurant, she is able to make relaxed small talk with the waiters because she feels at home in an upscale environment. I know that she is in college in Lund, sometimes he comes out with things without thinking, even though I've said I don't want to know anything about his family. Apparently she is studying political science, something to do with international politics, I know nothing about that kind of thing. I'm sure she's one of those people who will end up with a fantastic job in the Foreign Office or the United Nations or the Swedish International Development Cooperation Agency after several years studying abroad and a series of highly desirable placements, something amazing and important, she will speak several languages fluently and she will never feel nervous when it comes to ordering in a restaurant. I'm sure he's proud of her. I want him to be proud of me too. I want to find ways of making him proud.

He won't text me, he never does on evenings like this. They will drink expensive wine with the meal, perhaps Cognac with their coffee, the bill will run to thousands, but that's just a small part of her present, I try to imagine what Sandra Malmberg will want for her birthday. Clothes, maybe, or a designer purse. Carl has probably been involved in choosing her present, he likes doing that kind of thing, he's unusually interested in fashion for a man in his fifties. I picture him handing her a beautifully wrapped, costly gift that he has picked out himself, and he has chosen exactly the right thing, he has bought a fabulous item of clothing which will attract compliments from all her friends, who also receive expensive birthday presents from their daddies.

I have fantasized about his wife dying. It happens in brief moments before my brain realizes what it is doing, and I immediately feel ashamed of myself and have to try to cleanse it, wash away the terrible thought with a flood of *I didn't mean it!*, just in case fate or God happens to be there, reading my mind. It is wrong to wish another person dead, I tell myself sternly, but still the thought comes back to me. It would be enough if she left him, actually. If she met someone else on one of her vacations. But it's hard to imagine that any woman would leave Carl, that anyone else could seem better in comparison with him. An accident would be best. Instantaneous death, even in my darkest fantasies I don't want her to suffer, I just want her to disappear. The worst thing would be if she got sick, because then he would have to take care of her. I hope she will stay healthy until the day she forgets to look both ways before she steps off the sidewalk. It is wrong to wish another person dead. A car traveling too fast, she hits her head, there isn't even any blood. It is wrong to wish another person dead. Death is instantaneous. It is wrong to... Then she is gone.

Sometimes at night I picture them going to bed together. She is wearing a negligee, something silky trimmed with pretty lace, she slips in beside him, lies down close to his body, her head resting on his chest, just the way I do. She is in my place. She touches him the way I do, just like me she knows how he loves to be caressed. She kisses him, he kisses her back. He touches her, running his hand over her pretty, silky negligee. He thinks her body feels nice.

Revulsion grows inside me until I feel like I am going to explode, I feel empty yet at the same time I am filled with darkness, eating away at me like acid. The thought of his hands on her body keeps coming back to me, like a stake being driven into my heart. How can you do something like that when you have such an intimate relationship with another person? Never before have I known an intimacy like the feeling that exists between Carl and me. Everything is so perfect, so self-evident.

Then it's as though Emelie is sitting in my living room, a knowing look on her face. *You're mixing up love and lust*, she says sharply to me. What does she know about it? She can't possibly be right.

I pour myself a glass of wine, quickly knock back half of it, look at myself in the mirror. My hair is a mess and my makeup almost nonexistent after a day at work, it disappears in the steam from the food and the hot water and the dishwashers, my face is pale and shiny. I am not even pretty. I am nothing. It seems so obvious sometimes, the inadequacy that is my inheritance.

I could have had the same kind of life that the other kids on the street where I grew up have today, an undemanding life, I too could have had a secure, easy job, I could have been married and pregnant and bought a house and saved up for vacations, I could have been one of the junior nurses at the hospital, then at least I would have a job, security, I curse the fact that I am incapable of living such a life, I curse my longing for life to be more than that. "Perhaps a normal person has to be stupid," thought Dostoevsky's man from underground, perhaps that's true, at least if you are going to find happiness in that normality, put up with it, be satisfied. I wish I could be satisfied, yet at the same time I despise those who are. I enjoy thinking, *At least I'm not like you*, even though the only result is that I continue to be lonely.

And then there are all those who manage to have the other kind of life: those who graduate from university and prepare their résumés and make use of their contacts and buy property, my body throbs with anger when I think about them, when I think about their self-confidence, the confidence with which they make the world their own, it seems to be imprinted in their DNA that the world is made for people like them, all they have to do is help themselves.

I have seventy-five credits in university courses that are completely useless in real life, the life where it is necessary to earn money every month to pay the interest on a loan no one will be willing to give me, I wear cheap clothes, I have a revolting job. I will always have to wear cheap clothes. I will always feel cheap.

I look at myself in the mirror again. I tame my hair with a product that has a synthetic smell of watermelon, I wipe the eyeliner from around my eyes and reapply it, I dust powder and blush over my cheeks, paint my lips dark red. I put on a black dress that isn't really clean but isn't dirty either, spray perfume at the base of my throat, that's the best I can do, but I've realized that men aren't all that choosy.

The Palace nightclub, glittering like a ferry that has drifted ashore at the bend of the Motala River, is almost empty at this early hour, I sit down at the bar, order a glass of wine. After a little while a man comes and sits not far away, when he looks at me I smile at him, he smiles back, picks up his glass of beer and comes to sit beside me.

"Are you waiting for someone?" he asks.

His Norrköping accent makes him sound pleasant, but slightly stupid.

"No, I'm on my own."

He nods. This is not the kind of place you come to on your own, this is the kind of place you head for with a whole gang of giggling girlfriends, dressed to the nines, after a long session of pre-gaming at home, this is the kind of place you come to with your work colleagues after a conference dinner when you don't feel like going home yet. Or if you don't feel like going home alone.

His name is Anders, he looks as if he's just under forty. He's an accountant. I have never met an accountant before. He looks like a typical guy from Norrköping, his clothes are nice but somehow boring, he's nothing like Carl, he doesn't have Carl's stylish elegance, he is more charming than handsome, he looks at bit crumpled and untidy, but the overall impression is pleasant. He's had a difficult week, he tells me. He works too hard, he doesn't have a ring on his finger. Perhaps he feels lonely going home to an empty apartment, perhaps he would rather go out and have a few beers and chat with whoever is around just to escape the silence in his empty apartment, I have no problem understanding that. I enjoy talking to him, he is slightly cynical in a way that appeals to me, he makes me laugh. When he goes out for a smoke I go with him, accept a cigarette so that he won't have to smoke alone. We stand side by side under the projecting roof outside the Palace where the ground looks like a Byzantine mosaic made up of cigarette butts and maple leaves in different shades of gold, we are both slightly drunk. We have to stand very close together right by the wall so that the fine rain in the air won't blow in on us, I am aware of his scent, he smells good, some kind of simple cologne, everything about him is ordinary, I have never found ordinariness attractive before, but right now it feels like exactly what I am longing for.

He is a perfectly ordinary lover too. After I have asked him if he wants to come back to my place, and we have stood outside my door drunkenly searching for topics of conversation to fill the time between both of us thinking that we want to kiss each other and actually doing so, and we have kissed our way through the hallway and into bed, he makes love to me in a way that is kind of functional:

considerate and correct, but not particularly passionate. He is not like Carl.

Afterward I feel utterly safe, I cuddle up to him, he is warm. I always cuddle up to Carl's back when we have made love, burying my face in the back of his neck and inhaling his smell. I have murmured "I love you" a few times, and he has murmured the same words back to me, half asleep, in the trancelike state that follows when I have done everything that lovers do, it feels the same right now. The accountant is also warm and he smells good as I nestle closer to him. "I love you," I murmur. It's like a reflex, the words follow automatically from the feeling of security that comes from being next to another body, I whisper them quietly into the back of his neck as I do with Carl, sometimes so quietly that he doesn't hear, sometimes he has already fallen asleep.

But the accountant has not fallen asleep. He turns over immediately, staring at me with a mixture of horror and revulsion in his eyes. As if I were crazy. Maybe I am.

"What did you say?"

I look away. "Nothing. I don't know. I made a mistake."

I turn my back on him in bed. I hear him sit up, sigh. Then he gets up, walks around the room gathering up his clothes, which are scattered all over the floor. He sits down on the bed, buttoning his shirt.

"I have to go," he says.

"Okay," I mumble.

I am drawn to the harbor in the evenings. I prefer to go at twilight, but the days are so short now, it is already dark in the afternoons when I am still sitting with Siv and Magdalena on our break, gazing out over the hospital parking lot as a truck carrying a huge Christmas tree pulls up outside the entrance. Siv thinks it's a bit early, and I agree, it's November, the clocks have only just gone back, perhaps there has been some kind of misunderstanding, but maybe those who are responsible for the hospital grounds think that anything that will light up the darkness in the ugly parking lot where the wind always howls is a good idea, that's what I would have thought.

I stick to the southern side of the harbor. The northern side looks more like an industrial estate, with ugly buildings housing firms that dig holes and fix drains, mountains of coal, big piles of timber ready to be sent across the world, to be loaded onto ships and transported and used in a land far away from here.

On the southern side there are cranes fixed to the ground on rails, like tramlines, they can move backward and forward along the quayside. A ship is moored next to a long row of containers full of gravel, in darkness, silent, waiting. Perhaps they are all asleep on board, the seamen from the other side of the world, or perhaps they have gone ashore and are sitting in some bar in town, or perhaps they are walking the same streets as me, looking for women who are walking the streets too.

If you walk past the cranes and the containers, past the storage depots and the sooty brick building that used to be the customhouse, farther and farther out, eventually you reach an abandoned ferry terminal. Back in the nineties ships were supposed to travel to the new Baltic, I don't remember where, Tallinn or Riga. Nobody used the ferries, and the plans were canceled after just a few trips. Nobody from a dilapidated harbor town wants to sail across an ice-cold sea to another dilapidated harbor town, they should have been able to work that out. The terminal is still there, a low building made of metal and glass, with rows and rows of red plastic chairs, still virtually unused beneath a thick layer of dust, the same red as the shipping company's logo, a deserted information desk and a ticket office. It has aged badly, the paintwork is flaking and faded, the metal rusty, the whole thing looks cheap.

The tower that led to the ferries is still there on the quayside, it looks like the tunnel you walk through when boarding a plane: a staircase leading up to a corridor leading nowhere. I have fantasized about this, watched it play out before my eyes like a film: I am walking up the stairs, along the swaying floor of the corridor, I am thinking that this is the route that will take me away from here, take me somewhere else, and then I take that last step straight out into nothingness, I begin to fall before I realize what has happened, I split the surface of the dark, ice-cold water, I am swallowed up by the water, which is heavy, sucking me down, dragging me down, and I sink.

Don't fall in love, Emelie has said to me over and over again. I have told her that I won't, that I will just be his mistress, I am happy with that. But it's not going to work, I realized that at an early stage. As soon as he was lying in my arms after we had made love, with me stroking his cheek and him rendered harmless, that tall, slightly stern consultant from the cafeteria was suddenly mine, he was naked in my bed with his head resting on my breast, allowing me to caress him. He fell asleep almost immediately, and when he woke up he looked at me with confusion in his eyes for a second before it all came back to him, and then he smiled in a way that showed he was happy to be close to me, he told me I was beautiful. He sounded grateful, humble. It was an entirely new feeling: I had a kind of power over him. And that made me submissive, almost grateful in return because he had given me that power, because he had the courage to be small before me. There was such an intense intimacy in that moment that my eyes filled with tears, and he drew my face down to his and kissed me gently and held me so very close, and I knew it would be impossible not to fall in love.

Besides, he is a good person. A genuinely good man: there is something honest about his whole being, just as

I thought the first time I noticed his laugh. He is decent, straightforward, simple without being banal.

I could live with him, I have thought that many times.

But how would it look if he got divorced? This is his second marriage. You have to think about that kind of thing when you're an adult. You have to think about the children and your salary and what people would say.

"He's not going to leave her," Emelie says over coffee.

She has said it before, and it upset me, but now it seems to me that she just doesn't understand, because she has never experienced anything like what I have with Carl, such an intimate relationship, such a perfect balance between attraction and respect and tenderness.

"He's too old for you," she adds.

"He's not that old."

"He's nearly twice as old as you."

"If we were in Hollywood he could be, like, seventy, and nobody would think it was weird."

"But we're not in Hollywood. We're in Norrköping."

She slurps her revolting coffee, which smells of hazelnuts. She could well be the only person left in the world who still likes those flavored syrups in her coffee, everybody else gave up after they'd tried them, or at least after they finished high school. She has bad taste, that's all there is to it. I suddenly find her really annoying, everything about her gets on my nerves.

"I thought you approved of everything that goes against the norm?" I said.

"Sorry?"

She sounds defensive.

"Well, you're always talking about how important that kind of thing is. The male norm and the hetero norm and the white Caucasian norm and all the other stuff you care about. But now I'm doing something that really does go against the norm, and that's no good either, because it's not the right norm, according to you."

"I never said that."

"Yes, you did. It just old-fashioned moralizing, because I'm in a relationship that doesn't fit in with your list of approved norm-breaking relationships. If I'd gotten together with an older woman, I'm sure you would have thought that was fantastic and totally liberated; you'd have been sitting here encouraging me."

She looks a little unsure of herself, as if at least some of what I have said has hit home, and that fires me up even more.

"What's the actual point of everything you believe in?" I say. I can't stop myself now, I have to get it all out. "Do you seriously believe that if you just talk about the feminist struggle at every party and keep going to your cheerleading group, something is going to change? Do you imagine everyone in the whole world is going to wake up one day and use their free will to want exactly what you think they ought to want? What's best for them, purely from your point of view? You won't be part of all that, of course, because you happen to want to live in a heterosexual relationship in a nice apartment in a way that is kind of radical anyway, because you're aware that you are the norm... Does that give you the right to judge everyone else?"

"You're not making any sense," she said.

Personally I think I've never been clearer. I am filled with a sense of having seen through everything.

"Niklas says – " she goes on.

"Have you talked to Niklas about me?"

"Yes." She looks surprised. "I talk to Niklas about everything."

"I'd rather you didn't."

"I'm sorry, but you can't stop me," she says in an unbearably arrogant tone of voice that is just too much for me. I have to go. I get to my feet and say exactly that. "I have to go," and I leave: out on the street I feel like a stubborn child who wants to scream *I can't stand it!* and I can't stand it, I can't cope with all that falseness. Suddenly Emelie seems to be the very incarnation of what I am talking about: people can become so obsessed with theories and structures that their whole life is nothing more than an attempt to navigate around them, they refuse to take off the blinkers, to understand that theories are *theories*, not truths, you can't just use them randomly in reality, you can't use the same tools in life as you would in feminist textual analysis or whatever it is that Emelie is into these days. You can't live according to theories. It shows a complete lack of respect for life itself.

The thought makes me sad and angry at the same time: with all the freedom Emelie has when it comes to self-realization, a freedom many people would never even dare to dream of – I am thinking of my relatives, of the cooks in the main hospital kitchen – and with the wonderful opportunity to let her life become something bigger, she deliberately limits herself, ties herself up with fresh restrictions on what is and is not acceptable. How can she do that, what a waste, what a privilege for the spoiled middle classes, who have every opportunity open to them: she is willfully making her life poorer by living according to a few theories put forward in the books she is studying in college, following them as if they were commandments.

I feel drunk with rage. I knock back a glass of wine as soon as I get home, then I feel drunk for real. I pick up my cell phone and text Alex.

"Hi, how are you, what are you doing?"

She answers right away: "Having a beer with some of the guys from my class, bored out of my mind. Want to meet?"

You bet I do.

We arrange to meet at the new wine bar by the theater, but it's closed, so we go to the Palace instead. As usual it's quiet early in the evening, there is no one else at the bar. Alex lets me tell her all about my views on Emelie and what has made me so angry, then she talks animatedly about her graphic design tutor, she still hasn't slept with him, but she's convinced he's flirting with her.

"I sit there at his lectures just feeling horny; I'm not learning anything. And now he's asked if I'd like to help out with a project he's working on, he's setting up an exhibition for the Museum of Labor. It's in the evenings, and it hasn't really got anything to do with the university, but he thought I'd fit right in. I mean, it's almost like saying he thinks I'm talented, right?"

"Absolutely."

"By the way, I don't think he listens to synth pop or rides a motorcycle, which means those leather pants are just weird."

We order another drink and I feel drunk and happy now, unlike the way I felt just an hour ago, and I think Alex is wonderful, at last there is someone like her around, and then I see someone I recognize out of the corner of my eye, it's the accountant.

I wave to him, it's obvious he's already noticed me but didn't dare say hello, because his wave doesn't look anywhere near as surprised as he probably thinks it does. He gets up and comes over. I am about to introduce him and Alex when I realize I've forgotten his name. He looks disappointed. He hasn't forgotten my name.

We pull up a stool and he sits down between us, glancing from Alex to me and back again as if he can't quite believe his luck. I catch him looking around the room from time to time, hoping that he will see someone he knows, someone who will be impressed by the company he is keeping. Alex and I are too attractive for this town, but to be fair the accountant deserves us: he is funny, he makes us laugh and he looks cute in his slightly crumpled shirt and jacket, he buys more wine when our glasses are empty, then he buys another round. Eventually all three of us are pretty far gone, and Alex suggests that we all go back to my place. The accountant looks slightly uneasy but nods: he thinks that's a cool idea.

Outside it is bitterly cold, perhaps the dampness rising from the river is creeping along the streets, this is how I imagine London in the nineteenth century. Our breath vaporizes, Alex's laughter bounces off the walls in the stairwell. The accountant is smoking a cigarette, he looks happy.

They sit down on my sofa while I fetch them some wine, I'm working tomorrow so I should stop drinking, but then again it's not difficult to load dirty plates and containers into a dishwasher even if you have a hangover. I don't have to make any decisions, take responsibility, achieve anything that requires concentration or even thought—in fact there is no incentive whatsoever to stop drinking, so I fill three glasses to the brim and when I walk back into the living room they are already kissing.

"Come here," Alex says, and I do as I am told.

The dishwasher down in the main kitchen is a cubist whale made of aluminum, lying on its belly with its mouth wide open, filtering dishes and containers through a series of vibrating rubber strips, stroking them into position before it slowly swallows them, washing and rinsing deep down in its belly, then delivering them on the other side, sparkling and red hot. Sometimes it feels like my friend, or at least my pet. I am its caregiver, I clean it and take care of it when it has done its work for the day, when the last containers have passed through it and been blown dry and the room is like a warm, damp cave, where the air exhaled by the dishwasher has misted up the huge windows against the December darkness outside.

It is my job to make sure everything is clean and tidy at the end of the workday whenever I am sent down to the main kitchen so that it is ready for eight-thirty the next morning, when the breakfast containers come clattering in, sticky with porridge, but overnight it must be clean, there are rules and regulations on hygiene to prevent the spread of infection among the patients. No one has actually told me about these rules and regulations, but I expect they exist, which is why the boss is so particular about the red mold that spreads like rust in the wet patches that form in the indentations on top of the dishwasher; they never really dry out in the damp air overnight, but turn into little red pools. Earlier in the fall one of the other temporary assistants had to stand on a chair and spray the whole top of the machine with the jet wash. Kristina, who comes in on a training placement for a few days each week, helped to sluice the murky water down into the drains. She's backward, or whatever it's called, not exactly retarded, but slow, of low intelligence, it drives me crazy when I have to work with her, mainly because it takes her such a long time to send the dishes through the machine, or to stack them when she is on the drying section, I have to work slowly to prevent total chaos breaking out, or I have to run over to her end of the machine to grab a crate of lids or plates that could have ended up on the floor if she hadn't caught it. It's not so much the extra work that gets on my nerves as the realization that I am doing the same job as someone who is stupid, I don't know how else to put it, and I don't know how to put it so that it doesn't sound unpleasant, because that's exactly what it is.

There are days when I think I'm being silly, that I won't be here for long, and that it's only the washing up I really hate, I have nothing against working in the cafeteria, and if I were working in an ordinary restaurant I wouldn't think the washing up was disgusting, I don't even mind washing up in the cafeteria, but down here, in the main kitchen, I can't help thinking about where the food containers have come from, which ward they have been on, which patients have eaten from them, what diseases those patients might have. Some of the smaller containers have been used by patients who can eat only pureed food. I don't know what's wrong with them, perhaps they can't chew, or swallow, or maybe there's something wrong with their digestive system. The kitchen serves tiny portions of different purees in the smallest containers, but they often come back completely untouched. I try not to breathe in the smell as I scrape the contents into the waste disposal: bright green pea puree, mashed carrots, something grayish brown that must be meat, turned into a mousse-like substance with a stick blender in the main kitchen's special diets section.

But there are some days when I think nothing is ever going to change.

I will spend the rest of my life scraping cold food into a trough, stacking containers and lids with an intellectually challenged trainee, wearing this ugly uniform every working day forever.

In the corner where the cooks hang out there is a large table with a stainless steel surface, that's where everyone gathers for meetings and breaks, there's a can containing the coffee money—you're supposed to put in two kronor for a cup of coffee, no exceptions, and there are sheets with recipes printed on them and a pile of well-thumbed magazines open at the crossword pages. The staff hunch over them during their breaks, or fill in the odd word while they're waiting for something to cook. One afternoon they are all discussing the clue "Sound alike," they turn it this way and that, count the squares, it can't be "echo," that's too short, so they try to make it longer, "echo effect," it still doesn't fit. When they've gone back to their pots and pans I count the squares: twelve. O N O M A T O P O E I A. I don't say it, because I know how they would react, looking at me and thinking it's weird that I could come up with that word, their suspicions overshadowing the pleasure of filling in such a long word. I once tried to explain that you don't have vacations when you're in college, and one of the women who washes up said that her daughter has a Christmas vacation and the midwinter break in February and an Easter vacation, and she's at Haga High School, and I said, "Well, yes, you get vacations in *high school*... ," and I realized she didn't know the difference between high school and university.

"Please tell me I'll get a different job someday," I plead with Alex as I sprawl on the sofa in her red living room with a glass of box wine. It isn't particularly good, but still it feels highly sophisticated, a real luxury, to drink a glass of wine, or two, or three, or sometimes four, on an ordinary weekday evening, Alex with her student budget and me with my low-paid casual work: we don't drink to get drunk, at least not really drunk, just pleasantly tipsy, tipsy in a civilized way, as befits the two of us. Every time we meet up Alex nags me, telling me I should write more, if writing is what I really want to do, and because writing is what I really want to do, I have obeyed her. I have written some short stories, I know they're not very good, not like Thomas Mann or Dostoevsky, but at least they're as good as a lot of other stuff that is published by new writers my age. If I can just gather enough together, I will send them to a publisher.

"Of course you'll get a different job," Alex says. "But above all you're going to write lots and lots of books."

She raises her eyebrows, murmurs "Cheers," and clinks her glass against mine before she takes a sip. She doesn't really know what she wants to do in the future, something in the media perhaps. Or she might stay on at the university and hope to secure a research post eventually.

"Your lover ought to be able to keep you," she says.

"I don't think that's going to happen."

"Has he said anything about leaving his wife?"

I don't like this topic of conversation, my stomach ties itself in knots whenever it comes up. I think about it all the time, to be honest, but I find it difficult to share my thoughts, even with Alex, although I know she won't judge me. We don't have to share everything, I often think. I have never felt comfortable talking about private matters, not to anyone.

"We haven't actually discussed it," I mumble.

"You ought to ask him what his plans are," she says. "If you want to be more than his mistress, you're going to have to push him."

"I'm not exactly the kind of person who pushes things."

"Then maybe you're going to have to change."

I make coffee after we have made love, it is afternoon, he is going to the hospital shortly. I don't have a shift in the cafeteria so I thought I'd spend the day writing, even though I know it probably won't go well, but if I sit at the computer with the document in front of me for long enough, then sooner or later I am bound to start writing out of sheer boredom.

We have our coffee at my little kitchen table, I really love having him here. It feels like we are a real couple, drinking coffee together before he goes off to work, and tonight we will do something nice, something perfectly ordinary but nice, maybe watch a movie, have a glass of wine, and I will fall asleep with my head on his lap on the sofa, thinking about it almost gives me a physical pain in my heart.

He clears his throat. "Are you doing anything special tomorrow night?" he asks.

I hardly ever do anything special. I shake my head.

"I was thinking... ," he begins. "I was thinking you might want to come out with me. To a private viewing."

"For real?"

He laughs. "Yes, for real. My wife is away, and... well, I thought you might enjoy it. It's at the Museum of Art."

A wave of affection floods my whole body. I have to get up and give him a hug, I know how happy I look. He notices it too, he smiles back at me. He's so gorgeous when he smiles.

"Is it an upscale exhibit?" I ask with my face pressed against his neck. "What should I wear?"

"I think most people will be going there straight from work."

"They don't work in a hospital kitchen though, do they?" I mutter.

He looks at me, still wearing that lovely smile. He has never looked down on me. He doesn't think I am revolting because I have a crap job. I love him for that. It's not that I'm grateful, but I like it. It's unusual, in my experience. I think about the fleeting expression of disgust on Niklas's face when I told him about my job. Just as he is aware of the importance of women's sexual liberation, but would never want a girlfriend who looked as if she was actually sexually liberated, he is aware of the concept of class. Even if he could discuss it at a party with a troubled expression on his face, it's obvious that he would never want to be with someone who has a job he finds unpleasant. That's the word he uses, unpleasant. Carl doesn't worry about that kind of thing, nor does he judge a person by those criteria, he takes people as they are and values honesty and directness, I love him for that too. I love him for so many reasons.

He reaches inside his jacket and takes out his wallet, then hands me two five-hundred-kronor notes. I stare at them.

"Buy yourself something to wear," he says.

"What?"

"Does it feel strange?"

"You giving me money?"

He laughs. "Yes."

It ought to feel strange, but it doesn't. No doubt other people would find it strange. Emelie. I see the women's tribunal before me, what would they say? *Whore*, that's what they would say. I laugh too.

"My other lovers pay better," I say.

He smiles, then pretends to look worried.

"That's all the cash I have on me."

"I need to get myself a credit card reader."

It is dark. I am waiting for him outside the museum, next to the huge illuminated sculpture of a spiral which has become a symbol in Norrköping and has given its name to one of the big department stores. People are beginning to arrive, they are mostly late middle age, chatting quietly. The lights of the museum are warm and welcoming. It's not a place I particularly like. Even when I was little and we came here with the school, I didn't think it was very impressive, it was just a box, a square building that could house absolutely anything. I wanted something magnificent: wide staircases, columns, a palace of art. These days I find both the building and the art inside pretty boring, but I'm still glad it exists, that someone devoted time and money and energy to building a museum in this cultural desert, then filled it with art.

I am wearing a new dress. It is a perfectly ordinary black dress from the boutique right at the top of Drottninggatan that sells Swedish designer labels, I know Emelie usually shops there, I bought it earlier today. I've never owned an item of clothing from there before. It is made of perfectly ordinary black jersey, but the fabric is thick and holds its shape, unlike the dresses from H & M that I am used to, it makes me stand up straight. With the rest of the money I bought a pair of perfectly ordinary earrings with imitation pearls, but if you don't look too closely that doesn't matter. I am thinking that as long as I look perfectly ordinary I can't get it wrong. I have put up my hair and I am wearing my high-heeled boots. I feel elegant.

That's the first thing Carl says when he arrives. He gives me a hug and plants a quick kiss on my cheek, then he takes a step back and looks me up and down.

"You look lovely," he says, emphasizing every word. "So elegant."

"Thank you."

He smiles, I smile back. I feel successful, like someone who can walk into a private viewing beside him without anyone thinking that I don't fit in.

"Carl Malmberg," he says to the woman just inside the door, she ticks us off on her list and then we are in the foyer, we hand our coats to a boy in the coat check before moving into the main hall where there is to be an introductory talk. It is packed, a low murmur of voices filling the whole room. There are glasses of wine set out on a table, Carl picks up two. Then we stand there side by side, sipping our wine and listening as the curator gives a short talk about the Swedish expressionists whose work is being shown. I stay close to Carl, I can smell him. People who see us will assume we are a couple. It's something I can barely handle, I close my eyes for a second and simply enjoy it, enjoy feeling as if I belong to him. I want things to be exactly like this forever.

We stroll around the exhibition, drinking more wine. Carl nods to several acquaintances, they smile and nod in return. I wonder what they think, perhaps that I am a friend of his daughter. A friend of the family. He stops in front of a large painting with bold colors, slightly attenuated human figures with 1920s hairstyles. I don't really like any of the work on display, but Carl thinks it is wonderful. He says just that, his tone completely unguarded.

At that precise moment I know that I really love him, and I suppress the urge to say that this kind of art is hackneyed and overrated. I want him to keep thinking that this painting is wonderful, because he looks so happy as he gazes at it, and this is a new feeling for me, a new tenderness, it makes me lose the desire to assert myself, to come across as smart. He is aware that I know more about art than he does, he has no problem with that, no need to appear supercilious, nor to make a point of expressing his inferiority in this area, as I imagine Niklas would do, I've met men like that, men who have to point out that they don't know anything about a particular topic, they seem to want praise because for once they are not pushing themselves forward, and by doing so they push themselves forward anyway, they drive me crazy.

Carl is never like that, on the contrary he seems curious, keen to learn more, and when I explain why I like a completely different painting in the museum's collection, a sleeping boy from the end of the nineteenth century, he listens attentively, looks at me, he is engaged in what I have to say.

It makes me think that we really could have a future together, but I realize that this is what people wouldn't understand, the fact that there is a fundamental mutual respect between us. He isn't interested in me just because I am younger than he is and he thinks I'm pretty and he likes going to bed with me, but because he enjoys spending time with me, because he believes in me, he thinks I'm smart, and that I am capable of achieving things. It wouldn't be like a Pygmalion relationship with me as his Eliza, it would be horrible if he somehow felt sorry for me. And yet I know that I have the potential to grow, I have been striving to improve myself ever since I discovered that there is a whole history of art and literature to master: I have been striving upward, like a flower growing toward the light, toward what is true, what is good, what is beautiful.

To a certain extent Carl and I are equals, I am more like him than any guy my own age, or any girl for that matter, I just love being with him. We simply melt into each other.

And I think Carl feels the same, because only a week later he invites me over to his apartment. It is Thursday evening and he is alone; this afternoon his wife and children and his mother-in-law went off to London for a long weekend, but Carl has to work, so he stayed home. A long weekend in London must cost more than the annual vacation that was the highlight of the year when I was a child, a week in a rented cottage on Öland, Gotland, or somewhere in Denmark, and I have to fight my brain to stop the realization from devaluing the memory of those summers, that was the only time we ever went anywhere. This trip to London is just one of the many vacations the Malmberg family takes: in addition to spontaneous long weekends they go skiing every February, they spend at least three weeks in southern Europe in the summer, then they have another break in the fall if it fits in with Carl's work, otherwise his wife and children go away, perhaps with a girlfriend and her children, they might go somewhere at Easter too, if only to visit friends in Österlen, this is a natural part of their annual cycle of events, just the same as celebrating Christmas or midsummer, I think about the beaches I went to when I was a kid, I think about the campsites. They were beautiful, the Baltic coast is beautiful. Just like everything else that happened when I was growing up, those vacations made me the person I am today.

But I don't like the person I am today.

That's not because of the vacations, my brain says, *it's because of you.*

They live in an old building made of pale, coral-colored stone. The archway over the main door is adorned with Jugendstil tendrils of fruits and flowers, the door itself is big and heavy. Inside the light is soft, with small fossils inlaid in the marble floor.

The building has four stories, and they live right at the top. There are only two apartments up here, two sets of tall double doors with brass nameplates. Carl opens as soon as I ring the bell, he looks pleased to see me. He is wearing a shirt and sweater, just as he usually does when he comes to visit me, but somehow he seems more relaxed, completely at home, an extra shirt button is undone, his hair is a little messy. I follow him through the hallway and into the living room, it is light and airy. A Persian rug covers most of the floor, there is an elegant suite covered in brightly colored cushions, and a beautiful coffee table with a big vase full of tulips. The bookshelves are packed. A tiled stove, a bay window with a view over the rooftops, a round room that I realize must be the little tower on the gable. There is a grand piano in the center of the room.

It's the most beautiful apartment I have ever been in. It looks like something from an interior design magazine, a home where beautiful, successful people live, which is exactly the case, of course. I stand in the tower room, distractedly pressing down a few keys on the piano. Carl smiles, moves behind me, plays a chord, continues into the introduction of a piece I know but can't quite place. He plays with confidence, with focus. Then he suddenly stops, smiles at me again.

"It needs tuning."

"Right."

"Do you play?"

"No."

"Me neither."

We go into the kitchen, which is also light and airy. Everything is so beautiful. Living like this must make you happy. This is what I want.

Carl opens a bottle of wine, pours me a glass, even the glass is lovely. Just imagine having enough money to choose the very best wineglasses, paying over a hundred kronor per glass for the finest Finnish design, just as you have already done with the tumblers and the day-to-day crockery and the best china and the cutlery and the coffee cups and the tea mugs.

He comes and stands behind me, slips his arm around my waist, kisses the back of my neck. Is this what he does with his wife? It feels cozy, intimate. *That must make you happy too.*

I wake beside him, it is the first time we have spent the night together. He is warm and his breathing is calm and regular, he looks secure and vulnerable at the same time, the whole thing is so wonderful that I feel a physical pain in my heart. He is bound to realize now, just as I have realized. He will understand that this is how things should be, that I am the one who should be part of his everyday life. That we can't go on meeting in secret in my little apartment where we have sex and perhaps manage a quick cup of coffee before he has to go back to work, to his family, to the grocery store to buy the ingredients for the dinner he is going to cook for his wife and children in their light, airy kitchen. He needs to spend his life with me, because I make him happier than his wife does, I do everything better than her. It is more fun talking to me than to her. He hasn't said that in so many words, but he has said, "It's so much fun talking to you!" with an enthusiasm which means that conversations with me are quite different from what he is used to. It's fun talking to him too, more than anyone else I know.

When he wakes up he blinks at me as usual, he looks slightly surprised at first, then happy that I am lying there in his wife's place. Surely he must be thinking that I have to stay there. That he must greet his wife with a serious expression and a "We need to talk" when she gets back from London on Sunday, then she will grit her teeth and pick up her suitcase and get back in the car with the children and go to her mother or a friend and cry, if she's the type of woman who cries, and she will hate me, and that's okay because I hate her too.

But he just says that this is lovely, he pulls me close and kisses my forehead, then says he has to go to work soon, maybe it's best if I leave first so that the neighbors won't be suspicious, in fact maybe it's best if I leave as soon as possible.

I can't live like this, I say to Alex. It's unreasonable. She nods, it certainly is unreasonable, it is unreasonable for him to toss me scraps of what I could have, it's like torture. As if I were a dwarf at his royal court, with him occasionally throwing me scraps of the finest food from his table, leaving me to eat with the dogs the rest of the time.

"Do you think you might be exaggerating just a little?" Alex says calmly, perhaps I am. I don't know. That's how it feels. If I can't have him, then no one should have him. I say this to Alex. I tell her I fantasize about his wife dying.

"I do understand," she says. She doesn't judge me. She puts her arms around me and I can feel a whole ocean of pent-up tears inside me.

I hate the days when the difference between inside and outside is too great, the cold blue light from the snow that has fallen on Drottninggatan and the warm, dry air inside the department store, the flickering fluorescent lighting and the hum of electricity, singing like a thousand crickets above evening shoppers in their winter clothes as they move across the slushy floors, they take off their scarves and the static makes their hair stand on end and their noses run and no one is beautiful, it's a day like that when I see them. The scene is so far from anything I could have imagined that at first I don't react to the fact that there is something wrong with it, it's like when you see someone you recognize in a crowd and your impulse is to say hi, but then you realize it's not someone you know at all, it's someone you've seen on TV. I see two people who look familiar, I'm about to wave to them but they're not looking in my direction, and then, half a second later when the pathways in my brain have managed to put together the fragments of information I am seeing, I realize that it is impossible, unimaginable: Carl Malmberg is sitting at a table in Lindahl's café, and sitting opposite him is Alex.

The sight sends a shock wave through my entire body. They are cheating on me, I think. They are both cheating on me, with each other, I have to lean against a wall, my body is suddenly heavy, exhausted, I think I am going to faint.

Are they talking about me? Is she telling him about me and vice versa, are they laughing at me? Is he saying,

You'll never believe what she lets me do to her... Do they think I will never find out, that I will never suspect that she invites him back to her cozy little apartment where he feels so much more at home than at my place, so much more at ease in her company, with her self-confidence and her straightforward way of taking whatever she wants from life.

I quickly slip behind a pillar at the entrance to the café, I watch them. They seem close, they make an attractive picture, like something from a French film, she is beautiful in the way that women in French films are beautiful, women who have a stylish older lover, I can see the whole movie in my head. They almost have an inner glow of their own in this town, it was obvious that they were going to bump into each other eventually, that they would hit it off, get on well together. As if by magic all the thoughts I had about his wife become thoughts about Alex, about his hands on her body, his thoughtful text messages to her in the evenings, his kisses, his caresses, his confidences.

It is snowing outside on Drottninggatan, big flakes of sticky wet snow, and I have to suppress the urge to throw up with every step I take, I cannot turn my head when I cross the street because my head is aching, exploding, my body feels almost apathetic, the blackness is spreading through my bloodstream like thick liquid tar. When it reaches my heart I will die, I think, and I can feel that moment approaching.

I spend all evening lying in bed, I can't even be bothered to switch on a light. When darkness falls the room is lit up by the streetlamps outside, a flickering light that makes me realize it is still snowing. Then my cell phone rings. "Alex," it says on the display. The shrill ringtone sounds grotesque, it reverberates through the room, I switch it to silent, I hold the vibrating phone in my hand. The glowing screen stares at me, challenging me to answer. I have to answer. I have to tell her that I know, I have to get the black tar out of my body.

My "Hello" is faint, she immediately asks how I am.

"I saw you," I say.

"What?"

"I saw you. You and Carl. I saw you in Lindahl's café."

She is silent for a few long seconds. It's over now, I think. Everything is over, with her and with Carl, it's over. Now I am completely alone.

Then she starts to laugh. Her laughter is beautiful, sparkling and honest, it seems to me that someone who laughs in a situation like this is crazy. Sadistic and crazy. You can almost see it in her, there is a wildness in her eyes, something unpredictable.

She falls silent.

"So you've realized?" she says after a few seconds.

I swallow. "Yes." My voice is weak.

"Are you angry with me?" she says.

"I just don't understand how you could do it," I say.

She is silent again, a brief, confused silence.

"You mean why I didn't tell you?" she says.

I shake my head, lying there in bed. This is what it feels like to be empty inside.

"I don't understand how you could do it at all."

"Do what?" she says. "You mean how could I have coffee with him?"

"Have coffee with him?" I raise my voice. "I have no idea what you've done with him, but I assume it's more than having coffee. How could you sleep with him?"

This time I think she's never going to stop laughing.

"Sleep with him?" she manages at last. "I'm not sleeping with him. He's my father."

ON THE WHOLE I was always alone, on the whole I will continue to be alone. Perhaps it is a childish insight, this realization of the incurable loneliness of the soul, this realization that we can never know another person completely. It should have come to me earlier, in my teenage years. But instead it comes when I understand that Alex is not like me at all. It is childish even to imagine that someone would be. I am so childish. I am going to stop being that way.

She calls me for several days and I don't answer, but then I think I might as well let her explain. I want to hear what she has to say. For the first time she is the one who sounds unsure of herself, not me.

"I didn't know at first," she says. "How could I have known? I thought you seemed cool, and you were. The rest was a coincidence. A sick coincidence, but now I think maybe that means something too."

"Nothing means anything," I say. My voice sounds so sarcastic that I hardly recognize it. "Was it fate that brought us together?"

I hear her swallow.

"No, but... you projected a whole lot of stuff onto me. You wanted to believe I was exotic, exciting, so that you would feel exotic and exciting."

I protest half-heartedly, because I realize she is right. That makes me feel childish again, caught out. She never told me anything about her father, the image I had of him was one I had created all by myself: I thought he was something different from a good-looking and successful doctor. Perhaps he was poor, an alcoholic, dead – anything that would have caused her pain. Then it occurs to me that that is exactly what he has done.

"But he talked about you," I say. "He told me you were studying political science at Lund, and that it was bound to lead to a trainee post with the UN at the very least."

She snorts, or laughs, a brief, bitter little laugh.

"Didn't he tell you I dropped out? That I hated it? Or how much we argued about it, that he kept saying I should go and study abroad for a year because he wanted to get rid of me, he offered to pay for everything, did he tell you that?"

"That sounds terrible, someone offering to pay for you to study abroad," I say sarcastically.

"I felt so alone," she says as her voice breaks and she begins to cry. "I wanted to come back here because I felt so alone, I wanted to live in the same town as him at least, and he wasn't happy because he has his new family, but now I'm here and he hardly ever has time to see me, and I feel so alone, do you know what I mean?"

I nod even though she can't see me.

"I know what you mean," I say quietly.

She takes a deep breath to stop herself crying.

"Can't you come over?" she says. "I'll fix us something to eat."

We are lying side by side on her bed watching the smoke from our cigarettes rise toward the ceiling light, the white porcelain globe shines above us like a full moon through mist, soft and milky white. A jazz record hisses and crackles on the turntable, as warm as a real fire. *You go to my head, and you linger like a haunting refrain.* I've never known anyone who listens to jazz. The filter on Alex's cigarette is dark red from her lipstick.

"The thing is," she says, turning her head so that I feel her warm, wine-heavy breath on my cheek, "the thing is, he's evil."

She speaks calmly, as if she is merely stating the obvious. I wish I could say things that way. I wish I had the courage to believe that the strong opinion I hold about something is equally valid outside my own brain, that it is worth putting out there so that it can take its place in the world.

I know she is wrong, Carl is not evil. He is the opposite of evil, even if he does things that hurt other people. Alex and me. I'm sure he never really wanted to hurt either of us. She is drunk, so am I. She gave me red wine and beet soup in the kitchen and coffee and more red wine in the living room, which is also red, the floor is covered in Persian rugs. Then she offered me a cigarette in the bedroom. It's okay to smoke anywhere in Alex's apartment.

She looks at me, wanting me to agree with her.

"He destroys everything he touches," she goes on. "He destroys people's lives. He always has. He destroyed my mother's life, and mine. Now he's destroying yours, and he's destroying his wife's by sleeping with you. Before long he will probably cheat on both of you with someone else." Alex shakes her head. "He's such a bastard."

I stub out what remains of my cigarette in the big ashtray lying between us on the quilt, then I clear my throat.

"But I'm in love with him."

Alex's tone softens.

"I know you are. They all fall in love with him. That's how he operates. But he only cares about himself. He's never cared about anyone except himself. You can see that really."

She places her hand on mine.

"We have to stick together," she says.

And even though I know she is wrong, I allow her hand to remain where it is.

It has been cold for a long time, the inlet to the harbor has frozen solid and the icebreakers have been plying back and forth, the noise echoing across the water all the way to the docks. It calms me to know that someone is making sure it is still possible to leave this town by that route. The open water in the harbor is steaming, a few swans glide along as if they are surrounded by mist, as if they are setting the scene for a ballet. A sailor standing on the deck of a ship that is unloading timber is watching them too. He is smoking, he looks frozen. Then he glances up and meets my eyes on the other side of the harbor, I think he is smiling at me. I hold his gaze, smile back. We stand there looking at each other. I wonder what his name is. There are Russian letters on the side of the ship. Ivan, Nikolai. Andrei. I settle on Andrei. He has dark, cropped hair and big hands, the cigarette looks tiny in his hands. All the things we could do in life, but don't do; just imagine if I went over to him. Across the harbor bridge to the other side, I could wave to him from the quayside, start chatting. We wouldn't have much to say to each other, but that wouldn't matter. His big hands would feel cold on my body at first, the sensation would make me shudder, but not with displeasure.

He looks away, now I can clearly see that he is smiling. Imagine if he is thinking the same as me. Perhaps that's how he passes the time in foreign ports, he gazes at the first woman who comes along and smiles. Suddenly my life seems hopelessly pathetic. It is focused on a few people in a small town, as if I still lived in a seventeenth-century farming community, and everything relating to liberation and self-realization and city life still lay generations in the future for someone like me. At least Andrei gets to see something of the world. In comparison I am a dork, someone who hasn't lived. My whole body itches as I think about it, I feel a sense of frustration, of mounting panic, my head is buzzing, I want to scream, rake my nails down my face, hurt myself. That's the kind of thing that crazy people do, people in films trussed up in straitjackets. I try to walk away from the feeling, scurrying along the avenue. The claw marks of the tramlines on the street. They are full of snow right now, they must have a special vehicle that plows the tracks.

Nothing frightens me more than the thought that it will always be like this; I am a nonperson living a nonexistence in this nonlife. It's just a phase, I think, as if I were the parent of a small child, tired of the hopeless child that is actually me, it is just a period in my life. Soon things will be different.

Can Carl taste the fear when he kisses me? I imagine it tastes metallic, like rust and blood, like iron. It is the fear of being trapped. It is the fear that almost paralyzes me on certain days, I travel to the hospital in a kind of trance: the walk to the central station, the bus journey, the corridors, the changing room, I see everything through a blurred filter, I am locked inside myself as I pour water into the serving counters, open the cans of pickled vegetables, blink because of the vinegar fumes; it is too late, I think, I am too late. Everyone else has already made up their mind. They are already on their way. It is only me who is waiting. I am waiting for something that never arrives.

On other days the fear makes me straighten my back, fills me with a kind of pride, the knowledge that I hold my fate in my hands and it is up to me to determine what happens. This is just a phase, I repeat as I print out forms, call university administrators, fill in applications. I too could be one of those people who continue their studies. If I don't write a collection of short stories and then several novels, I could write a dissertation. It's not just people like Alex who can do that kind of thing, people who come from families where everyone has been to university and got good jobs and fine titles, for that very reason I ought to do it too. The fear picks me up by the scruff of the neck: I will walk the university corridors with my head held high and my shoulders back, I will never think that I don't have as much right as anyone else to be there.

I picture the fear as gall, its blackness running through my system, seeping out through my pores, making me dirty. It could end here, the progress I have imagined ever since I was little when I stood at the window watching my parents go off to work just after six o'clock in the morning. Way back then I thought that I didn't want that, I didn't want a job where you had to clock in before seven, a job that was exactly the same every single day, a job you hated and regarded as a waste of time, a pointless job you did just for the money, a job that made your body ache with weariness and exhausted your mind, your eyes fixed on Friday from first thing on Monday morning, your belly full of anxiety on Sunday night. Every choice I have made has been an effort to move away from all that, and it could end right here, right now, and if that happens I am trapped and no one will come and rescue me.

And I feel angry at the knowledge that no one will come and rescue me, that I have no one but myself and never have had. That's the kind of thing that makes you strong, if it doesn't break you. Or it makes you bitter. Perhaps I am already bitter.

The worst thing is when he has said he will come by my place, and he doesn't show up. When I spend hours getting ready, wash my hair even though it doesn't need it just so it will smell good, take off my chipped nail polish and apply fresh, paint my toenails too. Then I sit and wait for him, with my freshly bathed, perfumed body and my soft skin, wearing his favorite lingerie under my dress, and he doesn't show up. Eventually my cell phone buzzes with a brief text message: sorry but he can't come tonight, he has to pick up his younger daughter.

My whole body burns with a feeling I can't quite define: anger, jealousy, the sense of being left out. The knowledge that I never come first.

I go out walking every time it happens. After I have hurled my basque or stockings into the back of the closet as if they were some disgusting animal I can't bear to have in the same room, a creature that must be locked away and forgotten, and after I have put on my perfectly ordinary clothes, in which I think I look perfectly ordinary—Carl would be disappointed if I turned up looking like this because he has made it clear that he appreciates effort, and that this is something he appreciates about me in general terms: the fact that I make an effort, he has even noticed it in the cafeteria, he has noticed that I wear makeup and that the lace on my bra shows through my ugly uniform, after I have eliminated every single thing he could possibly appreciate, I go out walking.

This anger is of a very particular kind, it is more private than normal anger. It is impossible to explain it to anyone else, it sounds childish or bitter, I can even hear it myself as the same phrases churn around in my brain, over and over again. *Don't I deserve to come first sometimes?* it says, and then *Depends what you mean by deserve, why don't you just end it with him if you don't like it?* and then *His children come first, you wouldn't come first even if he left his wife.* I walk past Strömsholmen, the little island in the middle of the Motala, Norrköping's Île de la Cité, where they could have built a cathedral but chose to open a dance hall. I try to think about that instead, they put white wooden panels on the sides to make the island look like a steamboat, then they danced through the summer nights in the middle of the rushing water, that was back in the thirties, it was a popular place, I can just picture it: lanterns lighting up the late summer evenings as the twilight draws in a little earlier each day, the dark August foliage, the moths dancing around, the lights reflected in the water as it races past on its way out to sea as a jazz band plays, it must have been like dancing on the *Titanic*. Then the dance hall burned down and the place was left to fall apart. That's just typical of Norrköping. The prettiest spot in the whole town has been abandoned since the thirties, no one is allowed to set foot there, it is accessible only to the random inventive homeless person or to drunken teenagers who force the iron gate and somehow make their way across the closed-off bridge to the island.

I cross Hamnbron. There is a gigantic anchor embedded in a traffic island, it must have come from one of the big ships that sailed from here long ago, when the harbor flourished, when strong men carried bales of cloth from the looms in town, ready to be shipped to other lands and sold. I walk past the first of the harbor stores, big metal sheds, nowadays they sell cane furniture and freshly baked bread, but just a few years ago there were swingers' clubs and gay clubs and underground clubs here. I don't know where they are today, if they still exist. I've been told that there were underground clubs all over the industrial zone, in the same buildings that now house high-tech companies and advertising agencies and cafés and university departments: the whole area was fenced off back then, I remember sheets of plywood and a thick black chain running across the main gateway of Holmentornet, the impressive entrance to the heart of town, the place was desolate in those days, but down in the cellars people danced all night. I missed it all, soul music could have been invented in this hopeless industrial town and I would have missed that too. I was sitting indoors, reading a book.

I sit down on one of the big cable reels on the quayside and light a cigarette. I hardly ever smoke when I'm alone, except when I'm upset. I shouldn't be alone. Someone who came first with another person wouldn't be sitting in the harbor at this time of night. I take out my phone and text Alex.

"What are you doing?"

She answers immediately.

"Nothing. How about you?"

"I'm out walking. Feeling angry with Carl."

"Want to come over?"

"Yes."

She opens the door, gives me a hug, and puts a glass of wine in my hand before I've even taken off my shoes.

"Are you okay?"

"I don't know."

I undo my laces and kick off my shoes, one of them hits the wall.

"I just feel like an idiot, sitting there in my sexy clothes when he texts me to say he's not coming. There's nothing that makes me feel more stupid."

I follow her into the living room, which is as red as blood in the subdued lighting, the thick upholstery mutes every sound. It is like being inside a body, a womb. It makes me feel utterly calm and safe. She sits down beside me on the sofa and asks me to tell her everything, so I do. I tell her exactly how I feel. How horribly lonely I feel when I think I'm going to see him and he can't make it, he has someone else and I have no one at all. Afterward he always says how sorry he is when we can't get together, but there is really no comparison, because he always has something else. A wife, a family. The tears are scalding my eyes. My whole being is a pent-up lake of tears, I am the tears that have been building up ever since I saw him for the first time, since the very first spark of hope that things could be different with him, that I could be different, that my life could change. Since the first time I felt tenderness toward him and thought that I wanted him to be mine. It sweeps through my body like a tsunami after a few glasses of wine, and for the first time I let it all out. So far I haven't cried a single tear over Carl, instead with every disappointment something has hardened inside me, like a sickness born of bitterness and pride forming a shield around my heart, and now it breaks. Alex puts her arms around me and holds me tight as I weep, I feel like I will never stop. I weep until I am tired, the way I used to as a child, although then it was over silly things, but there is the same sensation of inconsolable emptiness, and eventually I cannot cry anymore. Alex strokes my hair, her sweater is soaked through with my tears. Then she gently caresses my cheek, and my last few tears come from exhaustion and gratitude, I am so grateful that she is being kind to me, that I feel safe when she holds me. And then she kisses me on the cheek, her lips are soft. She runs her tongue around them.

"You taste like salt," she says quietly.

Her face is very close to mine. I smile, out of gratitude more than happiness, my whole body feels weary. She kisses my cheek again, I close my eyes. It isn't far from cheek to mouth, her lips tentatively find their way and they feel even softer as they touch my lips, but only at first, then they are hungry, she presses herself against me, the hand that caressed my cheek slides down over my throat and keeps on going.

When I wake up it is morning and she is lying beside me, looking at me. I have slept on her arm, and I turn over so that my face is next to her throat, she smells good there, the soft scent of warm skin. She smiles at me, brushes a few strands of hair off my forehead.

"I've been thinking," she says quietly, as if she is sharing a secret, even though there is no one who could hear her, "and it seems to me that we ought to focus on his wife."

For a moment I don't know what she's talking about, then I realize it's Carl. He has no place here, in this totally new intimacy between us. For the first time I have a no-go zone as far as he is concerned, a secret of my own, something that is mine and mine alone, just as most of his life is his alone. There is a balance now.

"What do you mean, focus on his wife?"

Alex gives a little smile.

"I don't know... but you often say you wish she was dead."

Before I have time to say anything, she starts laughing.

"I don't mean we should kill her. I'm not crazy."

She strokes my hair.

"I just need to work out what we should do. We could tell her that he's cheating, for example. We could write a letter. Even if he denied it she would still be suspicious, she wouldn't trust him for a long time. It would destroy something between them. Although of course it would make it more difficult for you to see him, because she wouldn't let him out of her sight. He wouldn't be able to come around to your place, he'd probably find it difficult even to text you. She'd check his phone. I want her to leave him. It's not because of you, but I'm sure you know that."

She looks at me with an expression of total honesty. I nod. I do know.

"I don't care what happens afterward." She fixes me with her gaze. "I don't care if he decides he wants to be with you when she's left him. I don't even care if he's happy with you. I just don't want him to be happy with her. Or with those kids. I don't want him to have that family."

I nod again. I understand.

I understand even more clearly when he is in my apartment a few days later. I am so disgusted by the ring on his finger. It gleams in the half-light in my bed, and I can't stop thinking that there is another woman's name engraved inside it, that it symbolizes a promise he made to someone else, a promise that he breaks over and over again, and suddenly this is no longer cool, or sexy, or exciting, it is just grubby and sordid. When he runs the hand wearing the ring up my thigh I think it is going to burn me, as silver burns vampires in the old legends, it is going to leave a bright red welt of burnt skin behind it.

"Her name is Gabriella," Alex says the next time we are sitting in the hotel bar, even though I haven't asked for any information. I have deliberately avoided finding out what her name is in order to keep my mind calm, but this stirs me up. Gabriella. It is sophisticated and intelligent at the same time. Women called Gabriella make things happen, and they are beautiful while they are doing it.

"I suppose she's beautiful?" I ask, it is stupid of me because I don't really want to know. Alex nods.

"Very. Particularly for a woman in her forties. You'd never think she was that age."

"Of course you wouldn't," I mutter.

"My mom is beautiful too. And so are you. He only likes beautiful women. But that's still not enough for him. He's incapable of being faithful. He's completely untrustworthy."

I know she's wrong. I can't tell her that I think I know her father better than she does, but at the same time I am certain that I do: her perception of him is based on childhood memories and a betrayal, she hasn't gotten to know him the way I have, as an adult. My perception of Carl is that he is the polar opposite of untrustworthy: he is reliable, considerate. On those occasions when he has upset me by saying he will come over, then canceling at short notice, there has always been an explanation, some practical matter that has come up in his life as a family man, I hate it and it makes me angry, I am crushed by it, but I know he doesn't mean me any harm. I have never doubted that he really does want to see me, or that he really cares about me in the way that a married man cares about his mistress when he knows that he can talk to her more easily than to his wife: not with the whole of his heart, but with those parts he can spare once he has fulfilled all his obligations as a husband and father.

I have never thought of him as anything other than a good man. So good that I want him to be mine.

The weather turns mild and wet, all the snow melts away. To begin with, rain falls on the icy streets making them as slippery as glass, the people outside my window have to shuffle along, even though they are in a hurry to catch their buses and trains. I watch them over the baking parchment, it is like watching an aquarium, although I am inside the glass instead of them. Black ice, they say at the hospital, record numbers of broken bones. They plow and salt and grit, the little orange trucks drive around all day in the parking lots, scraping away the ice so that no one slips outside the main entrance.

Then comes the thaw, and days of slush, pools of water spreading everywhere: inside the revolving doors, inside the cafeteria, there is grit all over the place. Siv tells me to clean the floor, I grab a mop and bucket and set to work. I haven't seen Carl at the hospital for a long time, he stays in his own department, but texts me several times a day. Alex texts me too, wanting to know what Carl has said. I feel like a communications center as I pass the information on to her with a feeling that is halfway between obligation and delight, I leave out anything I think is too private, exaggerate other things that I know will be perceived as being to my advantage. Then I notice Siv's irritated expression as I reply to one of Alex's messages, so I put my phone down next to the coffee machine and continue mopping. They will both have to wait until I've finished.

Norrköping in winter without snow, with no sign of spring yet apart from the longer afternoons. I get off the bus from the hospital up by the department stores and wander slowly around, out of one store and into the next. They have started displaying the spring fashions even though it feels like a long time before we will be able to wear those kinds of things, thin skirts and dresses, bright colors. I glance distractedly through a rack of items in every color of the rainbow, one section is red in a shade that really stands out: a chilly, strong red, like raspberry.

I take one of the red dresses into the fitting room. The lighting is kind, and my winter-pale body looks better in the dress than I had expected. I stand up straight, suck in my tummy and push out my breasts, twirl around in front of the mirror. It looks good. It doesn't look like me, but it looks good. Perhaps this is the person I ought to be. A person who wears a sexy red dress in the middle of winter, who tosses her hair and hasn't a care in the world.

I send the picture to both Carl and Alex. They answer right away, both of them. "Sexy, buy it!" from Carl, a longer message from Alex telling me that I am beautiful.

At first I am pleased, twirling around again in front of the mirror, perhaps I really am sexy. Or perhaps men always find women in red dresses sexy. Deep down inside I feel something that resembles defiance.

I don't want to give them this. Good writers are good because they don't lie, not to themselves or to anyone else. The same thing applies to good people. It's just a dress, my brain says. The fact that they like it is great, isn't it? But it doesn't feel great. It feels false. I don't want to be a person who tries to please others. Not the women's tribunal, not Carl and Alex. I never wear red. Who am I trying to fool? Yourself, says a part of my brain. Then I think I look cheap. It's a cheap dress, and the color is far too bright. It hurts my eyes. I quickly take it off, put it back where it came from.

You were both wrong, I think as I walk out of the store. People like you can be wrong too.

I have brought a book to the hotel bar and as I sit down in an armchair with a glass on the table beside me, I feel slightly ridiculous but proud at the same time: there is definitely something of the insufferable poseur about sitting in a bar with a book by Vilhelm Ekelund and a glass of red wine, but it's typical of the kind of thing guys who want to write can get away with. So I sit up straight, underline a few sections in the book. I would like to underline virtually every word. Alex is late, she has texted to say that the project she is helping her graphic design tutor with is taking longer than expected.

A man is sitting on his own not far away, leafing through *Industry Today*, he doesn't look like he's from Norrköping. Sometimes it's so obvious, those who come from this town and those who don't. Or at least those who started out here and have changed while they've been away. Apart from the fact that his jacket fits perfectly and looks expensive, there is an air of assurance about his posture and the way he turns the pages, a lack of self-consciousness that gives him away. If he glances up and sees me I hope he will think the same of me, that I am not self-conscious. That I am sitting here with a glass of wine, reading my book, as if it is the most natural thing in the world.

When Alex is over half an hour late I text and ask her if she is on her way. She doesn't reply. I do my best to drink my wine very slowly, but somehow my glass is suddenly empty and the bartender is there at once, topping it off. "The world is fire, become fire and you will have a place in the world," Ekelund writes, I underline those words. I will become fire.

It doesn't seem long before my second glass is almost empty and I realize I have been sitting alone in the bar for over an hour, and Alex still hasn't replied. "Hi, is everything okay?" I text her, I wait a few minutes, ten, fifteen. When there is still no response my anxiety turns to anger, an all too familiar anger. "Hello???" I write, I wait a little longer. No reply.

I don't feel in the least like fire now, I feel like nothing. Angry, and at the same time nothing. Just like when

Carl doesn't show up as he has promised. At least he lets me know. I knock back the last of my wine, beckon the bartender and pay, notice that the man with *Industry Today* has a plate of seafood pasta in front of him and is dining alone, he looks dignified. He must think I'm sad, whatever he thinks of me I must seem sad, either I was waiting for someone who didn't show up or I don't actually have anyone to wait for, I'm just the kind of person who goes to a bar and drinks two glasses of wine on her own.

Alex texts while I am making my way through the town center, heading down toward the harbor. "Forgive me but he offered me a glass of wine then we had sex" I realize it must have been written in haste, she always puts a period at the end of her sentences. If she had forgotten we had arranged to meet it would have been a different matter. That would have been acceptable. She has had a lot to think about, with an overlapping assignment and a project, plus the special project she has been helping her tutor with. But she didn't forget, she just didn't care that we had arranged to meet. Because she preferred to be with someone else.

I clench my fists so tightly that the nails dig into my palms, it is a good pain. They leave rows of half-moon-shaped, throbbing purple marks on my hands, I stare at them in the glow of a streetlamp, dissatisfied because it is not enough, what would be enough? I want to scream, hit someone, break something. Down in the harbor I kick one of the cable reels, that doesn't help either. My cell phone vibrates with a new text: "You're not mad at me are you"

"Don't you even have time for a question mark???" That's what I want to reply, or scream, yell it right in her face with all the anger that has accumulated in my body, it is like a battery of dammed-up energy, a dam that could run a power station.

"Yes," I reply instead, then I switch the phone to Do Not Disturb so that no texts can be delivered. Let her wonder. Then I think she might not even do that, as she's so preoccupied with her tutor and whatever they're up to. She has shown me photos of him, he's a good-looking guy, I picture him kissing her, they're both good-looking, of course they want to kiss each other.

But my phone is full of a long series of apologies from Alex when I switch it on the following day. Eventually I agree to let her come over and she apologizes in person, speaks in her softest voice, gazes at me with her most pleading expression. I tell her she is forgiven, and she is so demonstratively meek that I am embarrassed. On the whole I was always alone.

She reaches into her pocket and pulls out a ring of keys, she dangles them in front of my face, proud and enthusiastic, as if they are a present.

"I'm watering their plants. They don't want their fig tree to die, because then they might not be able to offer their very own home-grown figs with the chèvre at some dinner party in the summer, and that would be a real shame. They're up in Åre."

"I know."

They go to Åre every year. Carl likes downhill skiing, the whole family enjoys it. They go with friends, a little gang of beautiful, successful people with children who can ski and know how to dine in restaurants, they stay in the same hotel and meet up for drinks at the end of each day's skiing. When I think about it I realize how ridiculous it is to imagine that there could be a place for me in Carl's life, I try to picture the scene if I went with him to Åre instead of his wife: I would have to attend the ski school, much to the amusement of his friends and their sporty wives, I skied once on a field trip in junior high, and I knew back then that it wasn't for me. I would have to buy the right clothes, and when it came to the après ski they would ask me what I do. "I'm writing a collection of short stories," I would answer. Or "I'm studying literature." They would respond politely and with interest, but I would feel like a visitor in their world, someone who has come to take a look but won't be staying long.

The jagged edge of the biggest key looks like the silhouette of a mountain chain, perhaps that's what it looks like in Åre when Carl has taken the lift up to the top of the run and is gazing out toward the horizon.

Alex smiles.

"Shall we go over there? Right now?"

I have always found empty apartments a little creepy: it's like walking into a place where life has stopped, the ruins of an everyday existence. The Malmberg family home is clean and tidy, but there are signs that it was a stressful morning—shoes in a heap just inside the door, hats and gloves on the elegant chest of drawers, unwashed dishes with the remains of dried-on breakfast cereal in the sink, they will be difficult to get clean, today's Stockholm newspapers lying open on the kitchen table. I sit down and leaf through *Svenska Dagbladet*, Alex sits on the big sofa in the living room and puts her feet up on the coffee table.

"We could have a party here," she says.

"No, we couldn't," I say.

She turns around and looks at me. "Why not?"

"They'd find out. People would break stuff, or steal something... it would be a disaster. They'd pull down the chandelier or drop a cigarette on the carpet and start a fire."

"That's exactly what the daughter who's left behind at home while her daddy goes off on vacation with his new family would do," she says, almost to herself. "Attention-seeking behavior, that's what they'd say."

She gives a little smile. "No... ," she goes on. "No, you're right of course. You're almost always right. Good job I've got you."

Her voice is hovering somewhere between sincerity and irony, I don't know what to think.

She gets up, pulls out one of the big gray boxes on the bottom shelf of the bookcase.

"Want to see some photos?"

The box is full of photo albums. She takes out the top one, brings it into the kitchen and opens it at the beginning.

"End of the school year," she says. "That's Mirjam at the end of... what do you think? First or second grade?"

She holds up the album to show me. A little girl in a pretty dress is smiling at the camera, squinting slightly; it is early summer. Standing behind her is a beautiful woman with blond hair and a pastel-colored dress, she too is smiling and squinting, she has a younger girl in her arms. It is a lovely picture. Gabriella and Matilda celebrating with Mirjam. Mother and daughters. Presumably Carl was the photographer. There is an intimacy about the whole thing that I cannot bear: they look at him, he says something funny to make them laugh, takes the picture. They are a family.

"I don't want to see this," I mumble.

Alex slams the album shut.

"No. No, you're right again. Neither do I."

She replaces the album, then comes back and finds a jar of olives and a piece of cheese in the refrigerator. She opens the jar and pops an olive in her mouth, chews it with a thoughtful look on her face.

"We need wine," she decides.

"Isn't it a bit early?"

It is just after four o'clock. Alex shrugs.

"After work?" she says. "It's okay to start early if you've had a tough day at work. God knows my father wouldn't hesitate to have a drink at this time. In fact, that's probably exactly what he's doing right now."

She stands on tiptoe to reach the bottles at the top of the wine rack, which is built into the space between two kitchen cabinets.

"What would you like to drink, darling?" she chirrups as she pulls out a bottle, examines the label. "Amarone?"

"Sure... But isn't that really expensive?"

"He's no cheapskate, but it doesn't cost that much. He has good taste rather than expensive taste. Anyway, helping yourself to a little treat when you're watering the plants is part of the deal. Let's see..."

She opens a drawer and rummages around until she finds a corkscrew, she opens the bottle, then takes out two of the beautiful Finnish wineglasses. She fills both with slightly more than would be considered normal, then places one glass firmly on the table in front of me.

"Cheers, honey."

She smiles and raises her glass. The wine is delicious, possibly the best I have ever tasted. Alex cuts a piece of cheese and passes it to me, it's also delicious. Everything in this apartment is delicious and beautiful. I tell her what I'm thinking.

"They've got plenty of money and good taste," she says. "This is what you get."

"Can you imagine me in a place like this?" I ask her.

She looks at me.

"Yes. Yes, of course. You'd fit in here. Much better than where you live now."

It has grown dark outside and it feels cozy in here, it is warm and snug. Alex walks around lighting candles in the small colored-glass lanterns that are dotted all over the living room, then she switches off the main light and takes the wine bottle over to the sofa.

"Come here," she says and I do as I am told, as usual. She pours more wine into my glass, moves closer to me on the sofa, rests her head on my shoulder.

"I've thought so many times that I would have loved to grow up here with him," she says. "In this apartment, with all these lovely things, and the view. That's where they usually put the Christmas tree."

She points to a corner of the living room where it is easy to imagine a Christmas tree. A tall, expensive noble fir, its lights shining down on Carl and his beautiful family.

"I missed him the most at Christmastime. I still do. How sad is that? I mean, I'm an adult now, but I still think about it every Christmas, I can see him sitting here, with them..."

She falls silent. I can feel her breath on my neck.

"I've thought about every detail of his life. Not just about how they celebrate Christmas, but how they do pretty much everything. How they sat around the kitchen table this morning eating their cereal and talking about perfectly ordinary stuff while he read the morning paper, perhaps he asked Mirjam which books she was taking with her on vacation and she told him. You know, that kind of thing."

"I know," I say quietly.

"He's so fucking proud of the fact that she reads a lot. I didn't read that much. I remember him taking me to the library once when I was little. He was probably trying to be a good daddy, I mean it's a beautiful thing, taking your daughter to the library and showing her that you can borrow books for free, that it gives you access to the whole world and history and so on, it's like something in a fucking Bamse the Bear comic. It was winter then too, we'd had lots of snow and the weather had turned mild, so the sidewalks were covered in slush. I remember he wanted me to borrow books with hardly any pictures. I don't know how old I was, I know I was still in elementary school, I still preferred books with pictures in them. There were couches in the children's section back then, and I sat and started looking through a book I wanted to borrow, and the couch was yellow and he got mad when he saw that my shoes had made big brown marks on the fabric. I got so upset about the whole thing. I knew he was disappointed in me. I knew he thought I was stupid because I wanted to read picture books, and then I couldn't even sit on the sofa the right way."

She reaches for her glass of wine.

"But Mirjam... I'm sure she'll follow the path I couldn't cope with. In ten years she'll be the one with a placement at the UN, and he'll be sitting here with his Amarone, bursting with pride and telling all his friends. When they serve those fucking figs. It will be so cool for him to have a daughter he can be proud of."

She takes a deep breath, just as I do when I want to stop myself from crying. Then she gets to her feet.

"I know what we're going to do."

She disappears into the hallway and comes back with her purse, a big leather purse from the eighties, I really like it. I like the fact that she has it with her every time I see her, and that she would never think of carrying her textbooks and notes around in a rucksack as many of her fellow students do. She rummages around, then digs out a square object made of plastic.

"What's that?"

She presses a button on the side of the cube, and a lens pops up at the top.

"It's a camera," she says. "A Polaroid camera."

She takes a picture, the living room is lit up by a flash, then the camera hums and spits out a photograph. She holds it up and I see my own face begin to appear, the contrasts slowly growing stronger. It's a good shot, with the bookcase in the background. My face is almost entirely obliterated by the bright flash, only my eyes and my mouth stand out, it looks dramatic, like an album cover.

"Cool," I say.

She smiles, goes into the kitchen. I hear her opening another bottle of wine. With the wine in one hand and the camera in the other, she tells me to bring my glass and come with her.

It's dark in the bedroom. There is a scent in the air, I recognize it from when I was here with Carl. I didn't think about where it came from then, but now I realize it must be Gabriella's perfume. It is the cool scent of white flowers, I picture them growing in the shade, crisp and elegant. The thought annoys me, I am slightly drunk because of those big glasses of wine, and now I feel the anger surging through my entire body. It's as if I can feel her presence, although of course she isn't here. She can't even let me pretend to live her life for a little while. All my feelings of loneliness, of being left out, of never coming first are suddenly pointing in one direction, like compass needles that have found a new magnetic field. I want revenge on her, I want to hurt her because of everything she can simply take for granted.

I have flopped down on the bed. Suddenly there is a flash, Alex has taken another picture of me. The mechanical hum of the camera sounds loud in the silent room, a picture slides out, my face darkens quickly, developing depth and shadows.

"Good," Alex says, examining the photograph. "Can you take off your top?"

I laugh. "You're kidding me—why?"

"Because it will look better. More artistic."

I am drunk, but I still realize that this is a lie. She doesn't want to take artistic pictures of me, she wants to hurt them, Carl and Gabriella. I vaguely understand that this is the revenge. This is aimed at Gabriella, although I can't quite work out how.

Alex tells me to lie down, look into the camera, then she takes another picture. The camera flashes and hums.

"And your skirt, take off your skirt. And your tights."

She switches on the main light, I blink, I immediately feel uncomfortable.

"Turn it off, please."

She shakes her head.

"No, it has to be obvious that it's here. In their bedroom. It's going to be great, don't worry. We don't need the flash now. You look fantastic."

I reach for my wineglass on the bedside table, take a big gulp. She takes a few more pictures, then asks me to remove my bra.

"So that it will be even more artistic?"

"Got it in one."

She smiles, she knows that I know, even if I'm not very clear what I know. I do know that something is happening here. She takes pictures of my face and my breasts, the photographs drop down onto the bed like heavy autumn leaves.

"What would he want you to do?" she asks. "If he were taking pictures of you, what kind of pictures would he want?"

I reach for my wine again. Alex sinks down beside me on the bed. I curl up close to her, I feel a little dizzy. I shouldn't drink any more. She strokes my hair.

"Photographing you naked wouldn't be enough, would it?" she says with her mouth right next to my ear.

I shake my head. No, it wouldn't. I think of the present he gave me, the pink lingerie. He has asked me to put it on several times since then, and I have done it. I have opened the door to him wearing nothing but the see-through camisole and the equally see-through panties. It drives him crazy, he practically throws himself at me, he is almost violent yet grateful and submissive at the same time. As long as I can make him feel like that it doesn't matter what I have to do. I would wear whatever he asked me to put on.

"He'd probably want me to dress in a particular way," I say quietly. "He likes that kind of thing."

"Good," Alex says, playing with a strand of my hair. "How would he want you to dress?"

I swallow. I know exactly what he would want, but saying it out loud is embarrassing.

"He might. . . ," I begin. "He might want me to look younger than I am."

She doesn't even smile, she simply looks at me and nods. She's wonderful. I could tell her absolutely anything and she wouldn't judge me. I snuggle closer, I want her to keep on stroking my hair, but she pushes me away, gently but firmly.

"We have to finish this," she says, nodding at the camera.

"What do you mean?" I mumble.

She slides off the bed.

"Wait here," she says, and disappears through the door.

My glass is empty but the bottle is on the chest of drawers, and I get up to fetch it. I find it difficult to keep my balance as I fill up my beautiful Finnish glass with Carl's wine, and I also find it difficult to stop pouring. Suddenly my glass is full to the brim, and I have to take several large gulps to prevent it from spilling onto the lovely rug on the floor, I slurp down the wine, it is absolutely delicious.

The room is spinning when I lie back down on the bed. I fix my gaze on the ceiling light. It looks like a big pine cone, it is a designer light. No doubt it was expensive, just like everything else in this place. The only thing that's cheap is me. I have to smile at that, at the thought that I am lying in the Malmbergs' marital bed, besmirching it with my cheapness, with my H & M panties and my vulgarity.

I am still smiling when Alex comes back, she looks down at me and she smiles too, I want to kiss her.

"Come here," I murmur.

She obeys. She lies down beside me and kisses me, then she leans over and touches me, I press my body closer to hers, start clumsily trying to remove her top, but then she pushes me away again. She holds out a bundle of fabric.

"Here," she says.

"What's that?"

My brain feels as if it is made of cotton wool. I have almost forgotten what we are supposed to be doing, it already feels somehow distant: the camera, the pictures. Saying I ought to dress in a particular way.

"Put them on," Alex says.

There is a pale lilac top and an equally pale lilac skirt with a pastel-colored floral pattern, short and flared, it is made of jersey with an elasticized waist. The label in the top says 146–152. These are children's clothes.

"What's this?" I say.

"They're Mirjam's, I found them in her closet."

"How... how old is she?"

"Eleven. Nearly twelve. Do you like them?"

"They're too small for me."

She smiles and pulls at the soft fabric.

"No they're not. They're stretchy. They're perfect."

I swallow. Alex nods toward the clothes.

"Get dressed."

I do as she says. The top comes to just above my navel and strains across my breasts. The skirt barely covers my bottom. I reach for my wine and quickly gulp it down.

"This doesn't look much like art to me," I mutter.

Alex smiles, weighing me up.

"It's absolutely perfect. I told you it would be. Now let's see..."

She picks up the camera.

"Look at me."

I gaze straight into the lens, she takes a picture.

"Pull up your top... and your skirt, just a little bit. Look this way. Turn around."

I do everything she says until she tells me to take off my panties, I am embarrassed. She comes back to the bed, lies down next to me.

"If he was here," she says in a kind, patient tone, as if she really was talking to a child, "he wouldn't be satisfied if you kept your panties on, would he?"

She is right. I shake my head, run my hand up my thigh, reach under the short skirt and start to edge my panties down my hips until she grabs them and yanks them off, drops them on the floor. She looks at me and nods, I nod back. This is how it must be, I realize that now. The room is spinning, Alex picks up the camera once more.

"What a good girl you are," she says as the camera hums and the pictures tumble down onto the bed. "Now spread your legs and look into the camera. Excellent. Good girl."

We wake up next to one another, it is late morning, a mercilessly sunny early spring day, the sky is bright blue. The herring gulls are screaming, my head is pounding, the light makes it worse, and the gulls, my mouth is dry, I feel sick.

Alex is already awake. When she notices that my eyes are open, she smiles at me.

"How are you feeling?" she asks.

"Not great."

It is difficult to talk. This could be the worst hangover I've ever had. I try turning my head a fraction, but that just makes me want to throw up.

"Would you like some breakfast?"

"No thanks."

She looks incredibly bright.

"They've got a fantastic coffee machine. I could make you a cappuccino?"

"No thanks," I say again. I've forgotten how to say anything else, I can't work out how to do it, perhaps an important section of my brain has fallen apart, the section that links the realization that I ought to speak with the knowledge of how to actually do it. The bedroom feels stuffy, the bedclothes are hot, the whole room smells of bodies. I want a shower, a cool shower, but I can't even get out of bed. I fix my gaze on the ceiling light.

"What shall we do now?" Alex says. She seems to be speaking from a long way off, even though she is sitting beside me. "The best thing would be to leave the pictures around here somewhere and let her find them. Make it look as if he's tried to hide them, or as if he's forgotten. We could put them in one of his desk drawers, or the nightstand... but maybe she never looks in there. He might find them first, and that would ruin everything."

Only then do I remember what we did yesterday, and it immediately feels wrong, my whole body knows it is wrong. Wrong and sordid. My whole life is sordid, the realization hits me hard, yet in an abstract way; I try to divide it up in my head with all the energy I can muster. My relationship with Carl feels sordid and my relationship with Alex feels sordid, her plans to ruin his life feel sordid and the thought of simply carrying on as before feels sordid, the photographs lying in a thick pile on the nightstand next to Alex feel sordid. Mirjam's pale lilac clothes are lying in a heap on the floor, just to underline how sordid it all is. I wish Alex would open a window, but I feel too ill to ask her. I hardly know whether I'm asleep or awake. Perhaps I'm still drunk. I close my eyes.

"We could mail them to her, I think that's the best idea," Alex goes on. She still sounds far away, and when I open my eyes I see that she is over by the window, opening it. Perhaps she can read my mind. Fresh, cold air pours into the room, sharpening my brain to the point where I can get my mouth to cooperate.

"I don't want to do this," I mumble.

She immediately slams the window shut, the glass rattles. She sits down on the bed.

"Of course you do."

I try to shake my head and a wave of nausea floods my body.

"It's too much," I say quietly.

"After all he's done, you think it would be too much if his wife left him? It doesn't even come close to what he deserves, but at least it's something. A little bit of justice. You like justice. You're always going on about it."

Her expression is challenging as she stares at me.

In the best-case scenario his wife will leave him. Perhaps he will lose his children. She's a lawyer, she knows how these things work. She has to realize the photographs revealing fantasies about having sex with his own daughter are enough to make sure he's not allowed any unsupervised contact with Mirjam. If he is lucky she will handle things discreetly. If he's unlucky she will tell everyone who's prepared to listen how disgusting he is, perhaps he's a pedophile, I mean, what is she supposed to think – he'll have to move. He won't be able to stay in a town like Norrköping after that, he won't be able to continue working with colleagues who think he wants to sleep with his daughter. It could get even worse, she might report him to the police, there will be an investigation, social workers will turn up with concerned expressions among the designer cushions on the sofa in the living room. How will they explain the situation to the children? What will his girls think of him? Perhaps there will be a series of articles in the local press, perhaps even the national tabloids, bold black headlines about the doctor who molested his own daughter, that's what everyone will think. His whole life as it is today will be over. I never wanted that. I wanted him to realize that it's me he should be with, I wanted him to ring my doorbell and say that he needs me, I wanted him to kiss me and ask if

I still want him and I would say yes, yes, I do, it would be romantic, like in a film, what I want has nothing to do with the pile of photos on the nightstand. Now he will hate me. Everything will be ruined, for both of us. I need to explain all this to Alex, but the realization of what is going to happen makes my stomach turn inside out and I throw up on the floor next to the Malmbergs' marital bed as I hear the front door slam behind Alex.

I dream of ships colliding. Big ships out on the open sea, I am standing on deck and wherever I look I can see nothing but the horizon, the sky is pale blue and a little misty, it is summer and I can smell the sea. It must be a childhood memory of the Gotland ferry that my brain has found and made use of, because the sensation is familiar. My heart feels light, free, and the world is huge, the white ship plows through the waves, forging ahead. Then it collides with another ship. I didn't see it coming, and the crash is deafening, the harsh sound of steel on steel, the whole vessel shudders, I can see the impact spreading through the hull, the metal giving way with the same sound as when you open a can, the ship on which I am standing is split in half, it capsizes and begins to sink, I can hear a sucking noise as the sea drags it down. I cling to the railing to stop myself from falling into the water, even though I know I will still be dragged down if I hold on, and suddenly I am wide awake.

It is dark, my heart is pounding. My cell phone is lying by the bed, it is just after five-thirty in the evening. I have slept all day. The room stinks of vomit, and although it makes me nauseous again, I don't feel so bad. I am able to get out of bed and slowly make my way to Carl and Gabriella's bathroom. In spite of the soft lighting I look terrible, my makeup is all over the place, my hair is sticking out in all directions, and my lips are dry, stained with dark patches from the wine. I look old. I'm not very old yet, but suddenly there it is in the mirror, the suggestion of wrinkles under my eyes, a sharp shadow over my cheeks, which used to be more rounded. I am too old for this.

I sluice my face in cold water, swill my mouth with a dab of toothpaste. The shelves contain an array of expensive creams and cosmetics, along with a scented candle, I recognize the brand from interior design magazines, I picture them standing side by side in front of the mirror before they go off somewhere in the evenings; she is sweeping Chanel blush over her cheeks with a big soft brush, he is shaving, watching her and thinking that she is beautiful. She will throw him out immediately. He might have time to pick up his shaving kit, otherwise he will have to go to the twenty-four-hour store at the central station to buy a packet of disposable razors to take to the hotel room he will have to book into, because he has nowhere else to go. He can't come to me, because I am the person who has betrayed him. I can't even look myself in the eye in the mirror.

I tidy the kitchen, wash the wineglasses, and throw away the cheese and the olives which have been left out all night and all day, they look disgusting. Then I take a plastic bag and a roll of kitchen paper into the bedroom and clean up the vomit, I spray the rug with some detergent I found under the sink, then scrub it and open the window so that the chilly evening air pours into the room and takes away the sour stench.

I make the bed, tie up the garbage bag and place it just inside the door, then I sit down on the sofa. The living room is dark, through the window I can see people having dinner in the apartment across the street. A perfectly ordinary dinner for a well-off family in a beautiful apartment in Norrköping. That's what life is about, all that ordinary, secure stuff, that's life. Everything I don't have.

I call Alex, but she doesn't answer. Then I text Carl, asking him to call me as soon as he can, I sit in the darkness for over half an hour waiting for a reply, but nothing comes through. He is also having dinner with his family.

I feel empty inside as I mechanically close the bedroom window, check that I haven't left any dark hairs in the sink. I pick up the garbage bag on my way out. I leave no traces.

When he calls the following morning I tell him everything. At first he seems unable to believe it's true, then he starts shouting and swearing. "How the hell could you do that?" he asks, over and over again.

I know the answer: because he isn't mine. Because I was angry and upset that he had gone on vacation with his family, but perhaps most of all because I wished his wife harm. Because I wanted to destroy everything that is hers and not mine. For a moment I think I can't say any of that, how could he possibly want to be with me if I do? But then I hear how hollow my words sound when I say that I was drunk, that he already knows how manipulative Alex can be.

"I wanted to destroy your relationship," I say. "With Gabriella. I wanted to set things right. Get some kind of payback."

My voice dies away. How can I be so stupid if I'm so smart? How did I turn into someone who does something like this? He yells that I'm an idiot, his words seem to come from far away. He has never yelled at me before. Then he hangs up, only to call me back a little while later. He has calmed down and seems to have realized that it is better to have me on his side, that otherwise he is completely alone. When he speaks to me kindly I begin to cry, because I am exhausted, because I have ruined everything. Because I feel sorry for myself.

"Sorry," I sob, it is an egotistical apology, a final attempt to get him to be mine, to make him choose me, it is such a self-effacing apology that I might as well be lying at his feet, even though we are speaking on the phone. He doesn't respond.

When the call is over I sit and cry. I thought I had known emptiness before, when I felt left out because he always put his wife and children first, but that emptiness is nothing compared to the way I feel now that he has pushed me away because he is disappointed in me, because I have tried to hurt him even though I love him. When I think about that I no longer understand anything about what I have done, I don't understand how I could have let Alex into what was Carl's and mine. I thought she and I were alike, but now I know that I was wrong, not even the feeling of having been let down by Carl can unite us, however strong it might be, and at the same time I know that the only thing Carl is going to want is to save whatever can be salvaged of his life, and I cry even harder, until I almost throw up, because I am alone once more.

The dampness has crept in everywhere in town, it is embedded in the walls of the buildings. My bathroom smells damp. First of all I clean the drains in the sink and the shower, removing great clumps of dark hair stuck together with dirt and gray soap, breathing through my mouth as I flush them down the toilet, but the smell doesn't go away. I am aware of it every time I visit the bathroom, it has even sneaked into the hallway. There are no windows in the bathroom, it is a room full of dampness, impossible to air, just like the utility room at the hospital. I place a scented candle in one corner and light it in the evenings, it spreads a mild perfume of vanilla and sweet peas, seeping out into the hallway, but it is eaten up by the damp smell as soon as I extinguish the candle. I stare at the white walls, the grout between the tiles. The bathroom wasn't renovated recently, but it wasn't all that long ago either, I've never thought there was anything wrong with it before, but now I am starting to hate going in there. Normal people's homes don't smell like this. Perhaps I am the problem. I can't even have a bathroom. How would I be able to cope with a life if I can't even cope with a bathroom?

Perhaps it is my imagination, perhaps it is connected to the fact that everything in my life has been destroyed. Perhaps it is my brain's attempt to give a concrete form to everything that is wrong. In the interpretation of dreams, the home is always a symbol for the ego. I think it is my soul that smells bad. That seems perfectly reasonable.

I air my clothes, scrub myself in the shower. People can't smell of damp. Their clothes might, but not their bodies. I look on the Internet, but the only information I find is that unwashed towels can smell bad. My towels don't smell bad, it is coming from somewhere else.

At work the following day, the thoughts return. I have spent all afternoon in the utility room and am on my way down to the main kitchen to clean the huge dishwasher when it occurs to me that the job has seeped into my body, my skin. It has contaminated me. No one will ever want to touch me again, no one who lives the kind of life I want, a life where you don't have to spend your days in a utility room with staff who are paid by the hour. I have to get out of here. I have never felt it so strongly. If I don't get out now, I am going to be stuck here forever. My heart is pounding so hard it seems like the sound is bouncing off the walks of the underground corridors beneath the low hum of the fluorescent lights.

There are two white-clad figures farther down the corridor. When I get closer I can see that they are two men in scrubs, bending over a gurney. The contours of the covers reveal that there is a person on it, a man, judging by the size. As I walk past I glance at the pillow, where one of the men is just about to cover the face with a sheet. It is Carl. His face is gray, his eyes are closed, his lips colorless. I stop, feeling my heart beat even harder. Carl is dead. Carl is lying on a hospital bed, dead. Covered with a sheet.

What has she done? I think immediately. Has she come up with some evil plan that has gone wrong, or perhaps it has gone exactly as she hoped? How could she? What's wrong with her?

The men have started to wheel the gurney toward the point where the corridor branches off to the mortuary. I turn around, hurry to catch up with them.

"Wait!"

They stop, look at me in surprise. I am out of breath by the time I reach them, even though I have run only a few meters. My heart is still pounding.

"I think that's... I thought it was someone I know."

They stare at me. I don't know either of them, they look very similar, both in their forties, slim, fair hair, pale eyes. They look kind of dusty. Their faces are expressionless, maybe it has to be that way if you work with dead bodies. Maybe it is a mask you have to put on.

"Could I have a look?"

One of them shakes his head, clears his throat.

"I'm sorry, that's not possible."

The other shakes his head too.

"Patient confidentiality."

"I think it might be a relative," I say quietly. "I'm almost certain. Please?"

I am close to tears by now. The two men glance at one another, and one of them nods to his colleague, then to me. I move a step closer, holding my breath as he slowly lifts the white sheet covering Carl's face.

It's not him. It doesn't even look like him. It's a man his age, but there is very little in his face that reminds me of Carl. I take a deep breath.

"Sorry," I mumble, stepping back. "I was wrong."

"Surely that's a good thing?" one of the men says.

"Absolutely. Yes."

The wheels on the gurney squeak as they move down the corridor, otherwise the only sound is the hum of the lights.

I text Carl when I finish work, I am still badly shaken. He replies right away, tells me he will be going home soon. Would I like a lift?

I wait for him at the kiosk by the main door with a mixture of sadness and nerves. It hasn't been very long since I was standing here feeling nervous about seeing him, but for completely different reasons; it feels like half a lifetime ago.

When he appears I hardly dare to look at him, then I try to meet his gaze, but he looks away, and when he is standing in front of me I want to give him a hug, hold him tight, I want to cry and tell him *I thought you were dead! It was so horrible and I'm so glad you're alive and I love you*, but there is nothing in his body language to suggest that he wants me to touch him. He looks distant, wary. It feels strange, but the strangest thing of all is that there was ever an intimacy between us, an intimacy that was more important to me than anything else, and now it is completely gone. He is wearing jeans and a jacket, he looks good, as he always does, but there is something missing in his eyes, which makes him look old. Perhaps I look old too. I glance at our reflections in the plate glass window. Does it show? Can he see it in my face?

He leads the way to his car, it is parked near the exit and it looks dusty in the spring sunshine, it doesn't sparkle like a deep blue starry sky as it did back in the fall. We get in, but he doesn't start the engine, he just looks at me.

"Have you heard from her?" he asks.

I shake my head.

"Me neither," he says. "I think she's left town. She usually goes to see her mother when she's not feeling too good, so she's probably in Linköping."

"Do you have any contact with her mother?"

"No. Those two... ," he begins. "They've got it into their heads that it was my fault we never made it as a family, but she was the one who left me. I've explained this to Alexandra several times, but her mother has told her a completely different story ever since she was a child, so she doesn't believe me. We were young and we hadn't planned to have kids, it just happened. We could never have lived together, it was out of the question. I thought she was beautiful and exciting, she wanted to be an actress... We'd already broken up once when she found out she was pregnant, so I stuck around... then it became impossible. We both knew it, but she was the one who left me."

He sighs.

"How are you doing?" I ask.

"So-so. I haven't said anything to... to my wife yet."

"Are you going to?"

"I don't know. I don't know which is best, to tell her in advance or to wait until something happens, if something is going to happen. If I tell her and nothing happens, then I've destroyed everything for no reason. And if I don't tell her, it will be worse if... if Alexandra sends those pictures."

There is nothing left in his eyes when he looks at me, no trace of the desire that I loved, it was totally different from the way any other man had looked at me, a desire that wasn't only sexual, but now it isn't there anymore. He is not interested in me, the light has gone out. There are tears in my eyes when I get out of the car outside my apartment. It's over. It's all over.

I have used up Norrköping. I often think that I use up people, because that's definitely what I have done so far in life: I have had relationships that were like a sudden infatuation, even when it came to friendship rather than love, where I have tired of the other person, moved on. Nothing in my life is constant, I haven't known any of the people in my life for longer than a few years, apart from Emelie, but then I don't have her anymore, I have nothing left. I have used up an entire town. It seemed to me that this was ideal, not having any ties that were strong enough to bind me to a place, but now it feels tragic. Everything in the town makes me feel sad: the avenues remind me of Emelie, and the café and the area around the university and the student bar and the School of Art, the whole of the town center reminds me of Alex, my job reminds me of Carl, traveling into work and home again reminds me of Carl.

I search out new ways, streets that don't remind me of anyone, I take a complicated, circuitous route through town, but it just makes me think of the moment when I saw Carl and Alex having coffee, I turn around, take an even more circuitous route home, slink into a café that's only a stone's throw from my apartment, a place I don't usually frequent because only students hang out there. I sit down on a sofa, order a coffee, read a book, try to push away the feeling that everyone is staring at me.

Maybe they're not staring, I don't know. I've started to believe that they can smell loneliness, that it surrounds me like an aura, that they can see I'm not independent and carefree, having a coffee on my own so that I can read in peace, they can tell I'm here because I'm sad, because I don't have anyone to have coffee with, because I have nothing better to do.

I try to convince myself they can't possibly tell, but surrounded by their relaxed conversations and easy self-confidence, I become nothing. They annihilate me without even realizing, they are just sitting there, cheerful, secure, unconsciously excluding me. There is something naive about them, their bodies and the way they behave, their rosy cheeks, I feel old again. Old and lonely and pathetic for thinking that they have any interest in me, they don't even see me, they are fully occupied with their own lives, rolling along as lives should, full of assignments and parties and relationships. I am an observer, sitting on the shabby 1950s sofa right at the back of the café conducting sociological studies: normality, there it is. It's like being at the Louvre.

I have started rereading Dostoevsky's *Notes from Underground*, and suddenly I realize it's about me. "I am alone and they are *everybody*," the man from underground thinks. I have never read a sentence that I could relate to more.

The sky is light now during my evening walks, I go out every evening because I have nothing else to do. I have nothing left. It is a feeling that is simultaneously a bottomless abyss of horror and as reassuring as an old friend; I am an expert when it comes to being alone. I have always been alone, because no one else is like me.

The pale blue sky deepens to lavender behind the tower of the heating plant as I go over what I have done for the thousandth time. I am listening to music because it is light enough to see muggers and rapists, I am listening to the same playlist as usual, turned up loud to burn away my thoughts. *You took my love and left me helpless.*

Alone, the bass thuds through the music, alone, alone, alone.

Alex never answers when I call, and I have called many times, left messages, texted. I have been to her apartment and rung the doorbell, but to no avail, I have listened for sounds but heard nothing. I have stood by the door of the apartment block, waiting.

It is like Schrödinger's cat, but with compromising pictures: perhaps Carl's marriage is over, perhaps it isn't.

Perhaps Alex has mailed the pictures, perhaps she hasn't. Perhaps she isn't going to. As long as I don't know that she's actually sent them, there is still a chance that it won't happen, that she has changed her mind. I want to believe that I could persuade her not to do it, if she would only answer when I call, yet at the same time I know it would only provoke her if I tried. She would feel as if it was me and Carl against her, and that would be the greatest betrayal of all. Now everyone has betrayed everyone else. Somehow there is a sense of balance in that thought, a kind of justice. On the other hand, everyone is alone now.

Norrköping has an attractive skyline, I can see the chimneys of Värmekyrkan in the industrial area rising up above the rooftops, the outline of the Iron, it is all empty and false, leftover scenery from something that was once genuine, yet at the same time full of misery, now it is the opposite, false and cheerful. It is impossible for me to stay here. Whatever happens, this place is tainted. Get away from here, I want to shout to the ships moored at the quaysides, waiting to load or unload, lying dark and silent in the twilight, get away from here before it's too late, hurry up.

I get up and go to work. Above the baking parchment on my window the mornings are light now, the sky is high just the way a spring sky always is. A spring sky is terrible when you can't see anything hopeful about it. When the absence of hope is all it brings: here before you lie the gossamer fine days of early summer, the warm days of high summer, and they are empty, that is what the sky is saying to me, for you summer is a series of days that are too hot, too demanding, days when it will become clearer than ever that you are alone, days when other people go away and have new experiences and you are left behind, in a life that is going nowhere, waiting for something that will never come. I think the spring sky is sneering at me. In order to deal with it, I have signed up to work all through the summer. The cafeteria is quiet then, with a relatively small number of customers each day, and not much cleaning up: days when you can leave early if you want to, if you have something else to do, or you can let the afternoon coffee break spread out across the workday like a soft exhalation, until it is time to go home and do nothing in a town where I am alone now.

PROCLAIM CENTURIES OF SORROW, PROCLAIM CENTURIES OF JOY. Maybe I will be able to write over the summer, if I'm not so tired at the end of the day. Maybe it could be a way of making something in my life feel meaningful. When I get back from my walks down by the harbor in the evenings and I lie on my sofa with the TV on low, not caring what's on, some crime show, some lame sitcom, and I gaze into the semidarkness of the apartment and I haven't got the strength to do anything, I can't read a book, I can't write a single line, and it's because my mind is weary, not my body, I think that I should at least be angry, that I should write out of rage, out of the desire for revenge, but I don't feel any of that. I am empty and weary and lonely. I have lost everything.

"You look tired," Siv says, quite rightly, as I am pouring water into the warming counter. She is piling little packs of butter in Duralex bowls that are so scratched the glass is milky white, she looks at me with a concern that surprises me.

I make a face. "Boyfriend troubles," I mumble, the very fact of admitting that something is wrong makes tears sting my eyes: I have shut down any such admissions so far, I don't know why I'm telling her now.

She is looking at me as if she really does understand me.

"You're so cute," she says. "I'm sure you'll meet someone else very soon. Someone who won't break your heart."

My cell phone rings. When I am not cleaning up I keep it in my pocket, it vibrates against my thigh. "Carl," the display says. It's been a long time since he called me.

He doesn't ask how I am.

"Are you at work?" he says as soon as I answer.

"Yes."

"Are you working tomorrow?"

"No."

"We'd like you to come over."

"Who's we?"

I don't understand what he means. He clears his throat.

"Gabriella and I. We'd like you to come over tomorrow."

This is my punishment, I think on my way there. This means he's told his wife, and I can never see him again. And he doesn't seem to care. Perhaps he doesn't want to see me. He just seems keen to get back to normality.

I hear Emelie's voice in my head: *Watch out for married men.* Stupid, wise, uptight, lovely Emelie. I should call her, tell her she was right about married men. Ask if she wants to meet for coffee. Suddenly I realize how much I miss her. What a blessing it is to have someone in your life who makes you feel secure, someone who is a little bit boring sometimes. Someone who is just ordinary. I should probably call her and apologize, but that goes against the grain, because I feel stupid, and because I know she couldn't possibly understand anything about my life. I would be forced to defend myself, and I don't want to do that.

The stairwell doesn't look quite as impressive this time. In fact, the whole thing seems slightly ridiculous. Who lives like this? In Norrköping? Perhaps this isn't what I want after all. When I think that I want my life to be in a different place, perhaps I don't mean big apartments, I don't care about status, about what other people think. People have such bad taste anyway, there's no point in trying to impress anyone. I want a nice, pleasant life. I would still like it to be with Carl, but I realize that is impossible now. He greets me politely, without touching me. It is so strange not to be able to give him a hug, snuggle into him and pick up the smell of him, that warm, spicy scent that makes me feel safe and aroused at the same time – someone else has exclusive rights to that now. Suddenly she is standing in the hallway, Gabriella Malmberg. She is slightly shorter than me, with a beautiful, open face, lightly tanned, her blond hair cut in bangs that cover her forehead, a body that looks flexible and strong, it is obvious from her bare arms that she works out. I don't have the strength to compare myself with her any longer. She can have him. If she's the one he wants, there is nothing I can do.

She also greets me politely, shakes my hand, and says, "Gabriella. Would you like a coffee?" When I say yes, she goes on: "Espresso? Cappuccino? Latte?" as if she were a waitress in a café. Perhaps she is nervous, even though it doesn't show, she seems calm, in control. I say a cappuccino would be very nice, Carl takes my jacket. I am wearing the dress he paid for, because it's the only thing I own that feels worthy of their beautiful home, if only Gabriella knew, I think. Carl doesn't even seem to register what I am wearing. I follow him into the living room. There is a big bunch of tulips in an asymmetrical vase on the table, there must be at least thirty tulips, they are stunning. It looks like a fucking interior design magazine. The whole thing is a facade. The marriage, the tulips. He looks sad. Or tormented, exhausted. His face is almost gray.

The children aren't home, I expect they're in school, it's a perfectly ordinary Wednesday, perfectly ordinary for everyone else, all the people who haven't fucked up their lives. Obviously Carl and Gabriella both have a day off, perhaps Carl has one of his days off in the middle of the week, and no doubt she can organize her time as she wishes, as long as she does what she's supposed to do and shows up at her appointments, no one cares if she doesn't come in until after lunch on a perfectly ordinary Wednesday, that's the way it is when you have a good job. When I had to go to the bank back in the fall, I had to ask my boss for time off, clock out, catch the bus into town, stand in line at the bank, catch the bus back, and clock in again, it took hours and it cost me several hundred kronor, you never have to lose money like that when you've got a good job where you're already well paid, it's one of those injustices that eats away at me, like the fact that we have to pay two kronor for a cup of coffee in the main kitchen. I wonder if they have a jar full of one-krona coins for the coffee at the law practice, the thought makes me smile. Gabriella Malmberg looks at me when she comes back with a cappuccino from the expensive coffee machine in the kitchen, I wonder what each cup costs to make.

"I recognize you from the photographs," she says when she has sat down next to Carl and opposite me.

I don't know what to say. She recognizes me from the photographs in which I am wearing her daughter's clothes and spreading my legs for the camera. Is she saying this to embarrass me? My first instinct is a wave of shame, but then I get angry. I would never have ended up lying in her bed wearing those clothes if her husband hadn't cheated on her. It's his fault. Judging by the way he looks, she has made that perfectly clear to him.

"I must apologize for this," she says. "I realize it seems strange to you, but I hope you understand that it's important to the family. I have to know that what Carl is saying is true."

"And what is Carl saying?"

I couldn't give a shit about his family. He and his family can go to hell.

"That he didn't take those pictures. That it was Alexandra."

Her gaze is steady. Carl is looking at me too, there is a desperation in his eyes that reminds me of his desperation when we lay in my bed, when he ran his hand over the cheap silky lingerie he had bought me and asked me to be his little girl. Although then it came from arousal.

The apartment is totally silent, the whole building is silent. Even the herring gulls are silent.

"Yes, it was Alex who took them," I say. "When she came over to water your plants. I came with her, we had a couple of glasses of wine, and... well, you could say things got a little out of hand. That was when she took the pictures."

There is no mistaking the relief that sweeps over Carl's face. Gabriella also looks relieved, although she is better at controlling herself. She clears her throat.

"Okay," she says. "Okay, so that's what happened. We would appreciate it if..." She clears her throat again, reaches for a sheet of paper lying on the table, pushes it across to me. "If we could agree that you won't tell anyone else about this. And that if there are copies of the pictures, or more pictures, you won't show them to anyone; you will destroy them."

I think she must be joking, but she looks perfectly serious. Businesslike.

"We were thinking of one hundred thousand kronor. Is that a sum you would find acceptable?"

"We were also thinking..." Carl glances at his wife before he goes on, she gives a slight nod. "We were thinking we could help you out if you wanted to move to Stockholm in the fall... I know you've mentioned the idea."

"Help me out? What, drive a truck with my furniture or something?"

I laugh a little, more of a snort really, but Gabriella and Carl are not smiling.

"A friend of ours is living abroad, and won't be back for at least another year," Gabriella explains. "It's a three-room apartment on Sankt Eriksplan. It won't cost you a thing, and it's available from early summer."

She pushes the sheet of paper even closer, it is a contract. I can hardly read what it says, my head is all over the place. They want to buy me. They want to pay me to keep quiet, then they want to send me away, just as serving girls were sent away in the old days when they fell pregnant by their lord and master, to give birth somewhere else and not cause any trouble. I feel disgusted. And cheap, as usual I feel cheap, and then it strikes me that a hundred thousand isn't all that cheap. A hundred thousand to hold on to the happy family, the Christmas card family. The serving girls didn't get paid, or not very much anyway. They kept on being serving girls. I wouldn't have to do that. I could stop cleaning and I could move to Stockholm, I wouldn't need a student loan, and maybe I could spend a few months just writing, maybe I could do that right now, over the summer: no more work, no more coming home with aching shoulders and feet and knees, I could just write, get up in the morning, sit down at my computer and write. It is a dizzying thought.

And suddenly I have exactly the same feeling as when I sat in the car with Carl, that evening when it was raining and he said my apartment looked cozy and I asked him if he wanted to come in: the feeling that I am holding my future in my hands in exactly the same way, that right now I can decide whether I want my life to change or not. I thought it was Carl who was going to change my life, and now he is doing just that, even if it's a million miles from the way I imagined it would happen.

I look up, meet Gabriella's eyes, then Carl's.

"Okay," I say. "That sounds good."

Back out on the street I want to laugh. I have seen through them. *You're lying!* I want to yell, like a crazy woman. *You're all lying!* Your fantastic lives are nothing but lies, your marriage is a fraud, I've seen through it! I can see right through you!

I have to sit down on a bench in the park among the alcoholics and the young moms on maternity leave, I squint as I look into the spring sunshine and digest what has just happened.

"It might take a couple of days because we have different banks, but the money should be in your account by the day after tomorrow at the latest," I hear Gabriella's soft, well-modulated voice in my head. She has won. She had won right from the start, and now she has sealed her victory, not only can she get a man that other women want, but when someone threatens her family idyll she can buy off her rivals. She will always have everything.

I don't understand how people who don't feel alone can live.

What part of your souls have you hocked? How did you choose? What was the easiest thing to dump: your integrity, or the need to share your life with someone on the same intellectual level or someone with a sense of humor or someone who shares your view of the world?

Do you miss it? Does it feel good to be a part of your particular club, so good that it was worth it? Do you just avoid thinking about it? Because that's the easiest way, or because you don't really need to think, because people who are happy *are* a little more stupid.

I am becoming bitter. It's me and the man from underground against the world.

I want to open my window to the light spring evening and ask the people who are drifting past in groups on the way to parties or to a bar where they can sit outside, they will have to keep their jackets on and stay close to the infrared heaters, but this evening they will be able to drink their slightly too cold rosé wine outdoors.

I miss both Carl and Alex so much that it hurts. It really hurts in every part of my body but mostly in my stomach, it makes me feel sick, and my heart hurts, or my soul, I don't really know what it is that is sitting in my chest screaming with pain, weighing down on my lungs and making it difficult to breathe. I had two people who were like me, and now I have no one. Perhaps order has been restored. I don't need other people. I have always got by on my own, everything I have done I have achieved on my own. On the whole I was always alone. I will be alone forever now, that's just the way it has to be.

As soon as I have reached that conclusion, my phone buzzes. A text from Emelie. I'm not sure whether to open it.

"Hi, it doesn't feel right having a party without inviting you, I don't know if you have other plans / if you even want to come, but we're at Niklas's place right now. I'd really like it if you came."

I am touched, surprised that I feel that way, that I almost have tears in my eyes. Of course I don't have other plans. It's been a long time since I went to a party.

"Hi, great to hear from you, I'd love to come but I don't have any wine?"

"We've got wine. Just bring yourself."

The twilight lasts for ages and the sky above the chimneys of the industrial area looks unreal, like a watercolor painting, the buds on the trees and bushes swell with every shower of rain, the birches are already in leaf, soon the lilacs will blossom.

Niklas's beautiful apartment is now Emelie's beautiful apartment too, she has moved in with him, that's why they're having a party. The place looks better now that Emelie's things are mixed with his, and they make an attractive couple, they both look happy and perhaps they really *are* happy, perhaps they think that the person they are standing beside as they greet their guests and offer them a glass of sparkling wine is the very best person they could imagine standing beside at a party, the very best person to be the other half of a couple. Presumably Niklas is exactly what Emelie has wanted all her life: a good-looking guy with plenty of money, who in a passive-aggressive, slightly bullying way is aware of injustices and power structures, and is able to lecture her on them while at the same time showing a certain level of humility about his own privileges as a white heterosexual middle-class male.

I thank him as he hands me a champagne flute and he smiles and says he's glad I was able to come, maybe he really is glad, for Emelie's sake at least, because Emelie will be pleased that I am here, because he loves her and wants her to be happy, but he looks fake as he says it, he always looks fake.

I have always found it impossible to go along with social games like this, with the kind of behavior that demands falseness. I feel dirty as soon as I say just one word that feels false in my mouth. It seems to me that it will jar, that people will stare at me, that they will know: does she really think we're going to fall for that? And yet I find people who *don't* dissemble difficult too, people who are determined to say exactly what they think at all costs, even if it makes the situation uncomfortable for others. Or those who have the attitude that everyone must take them as they are, and should value them precisely because they are honest and say what they think. People. There are not many who meet with my approval.

In the kitchen there are trays of canapés and bowls of chips, people are laughing and talking, the high spring sky outside makes them relaxed and noisy. It was at a party just like this when I spoke to Alex for the first time back in the fall, it's only just over six months ago. It's only just over six months since I met her and Carl, and thought they would make everything different.

I take a sip of wine, it's good, better than the wine that's usually on offer at this kind of party, in fact there isn't usually any wine at all, because they're all students and no one has any money. Suddenly Emelie is by my side, she looks happy.

"I really meant it when I said I was pleased you could come," she says quietly.

"Me too."

"How are you doing?"

How am I doing? I don't know. Not great. I swallow.

"Do you really want to know?"

She nods. Behind her there is the sound of loud laughter from the living room.

"Can we go outside for a little while?" I say.

"Okay." She sounds confused, then she seems to understand that I am serious. "Sure we can," she adds.

We sit on the rack that's used for beating rugs in the courtyard. It makes me feel like a teenager, so much so that I dig a crumpled packet of cigarettes out of my purse. For once Emelie wants one too, so we sit there smoking, in silence at first, and then I start to talk. I tell her everything, from start to finish. I tell her about Carl and Alex and everything that happened before I found out he was her father and everything that happened afterward, about the accountant and the photographs, about the meeting with Carl and Gabriella, and the contract and the money and the apartment.

"Oh my God," Emelie says when I finally stop talking. "Can I have another cigarette?"

I laugh, she laughs too. It's like when we were in high school, sitting and smoking in a courtyard just like this, waiting for life to begin. And just like back then, I don't feel the need to defend myself. Emelie simply listens.

"So what are you going to do now?" she asks.

I sigh. "I guess I'll probably move. I can't stay here. I don't really know what I'm going to do, but... well, I'll soon have somewhere to live in Stockholm."

She nods.

"Forgive me for asking, but doesn't it feel... doesn't it feel kind of immoral? This business with the money?"

"Morals are for those who can afford them," I say.

She gives me a wry smile. "Come on, this is me you're talking to."

"Okay, but what about this apartment?" I say, nodding up at the windows and the balcony door, open to the spring evening, the music drifting out into the twilight. "It must have cost a whole lot more than a hundred thousand. A million? Two? Have you earned enough money to buy a share of Niklas's apartment?"

"Of course not."

We sit in silence.

"You were right about married men," I say.

"There you go, at least I'm right about some things," she says, and now she is smiling.

The darkness as I am walking home is a spring darkness: light, kind of transparent, unlike the darkness of late summer and fall, which feels dense, impenetrable. It can't really be that way, surely darkness is just darkness, but that's the way it feels, and I don't think it's because I know it's the end of April. I think that if I had been locked away somewhere with no knowledge of time or the passage of the seasons, and I was suddenly let out into this night and could see only the sky, I would still know that this was a spring sky.

When I am standing outside my door rummaging for my keys in my purse, it occurs to me that I forgot to check the mail today, and in the mailbox in the hallway there is a white envelope, it is from the University of Stockholm. At first I think it must be a mistake, because why would they contact me, but as I rip open the envelope with the jagged edge of my key, I remember that I applied for a place in a summer course. It was back in the winter, when Alex kept telling me over and over again that I am not doomed to spend the rest of my life washing dishes, when with a rare burst of self-confidence I applied for several summer courses, just to test the water, to give it a go, to claim my place in the world in some symbolic way.

The lighting is poor, but I can still read the words with perfect clarity: "You have been accepted to Landscape as Memory, Narrative, and Construct, Department of Literary Studies, 15 credits, full time."

I have to read it again and again, and it really does say that I have been accepted. No "Unfortunately…" No congratulations either, universities don't congratulate people on getting into their classes, they merely inform me that I need to attend registration in June. Which isn't far away.

I have no doubt that Landscape as Memory, Narrative, and Construct is a crap course, perhaps hardly anyone applied, it's probably based on those French philosophers that Niklas likes, the very sight of the word "construct" annoys me slightly. I hate the fact that everything is a construct and I can't think of anything in the world that is more real than landscape, but still I am smiling: this time I will have the courage to open my mouth when they say something I don't agree with, I will raise objections if I have objections. And after all, landscape and literature are two of the things I love best.

The sky is even more transparent now. In my apartment I lie on my back on the bed and gaze at it above the baking parchment, it suddenly seems to me that it has regained its optimism, that it is glimmering, full of promise. I am going to move away from here. To an apartment that will be much, much bigger than this one, with blinds that work and a bathroom that doesn't smell of damp.

I reach for my phone and write a message: "Have got a place in a summer class in literature. It starts in June, so I will be moving to Stockholm then." I don't know what else to say, I add a smiley face but it looks a bit silly so I delete it, but then the message looks so abrupt, you can't tell if the tone is angry or happy, so I put the smiley back in even if it is stupid. Then I scroll down my contacts list until I find Carl, and press Send.

My phone buzzes after only a minute or so. He doesn't usually respond to texts right away. Perhaps he's having trouble sleeping, perhaps he's been called into work because of some emergency.

"I'm so proud of you," his reply says.

Outside my window the sky has begun to grow light.